SODOM
AND
BEGORRAH

PHIL O'KEEFFE

MINERVA PRESS
MONTREUX LONDON WASHINGTON

ISBN 1 85863 895 X

First Published 1995 by
MINERVA PRESS
1 Cromwell Place
London SW7 2JE

Printed in Great Britain by
Antony Rowe Ltd, Chippenham, Wiltshire

SODOM AND BEGORRAH

I dedicate this collection to the peoples of Ireland and Israel. They have wept more and laughed more than most races.

May their tears soon be dried and their laughter increase.

Contents

The Cross Irishman 11

Gratitude 13

Purged 15

An Saoi – Hockum – Man Of Wisdom 17

The Parting 19

A Family Affair 20

The Grafter 22

Yiddishe Koph 23

What's In A Name? 25

Different Tastes 26

The Home Lover 27

The Hod Carrier 28

Doubting Manny 29

Seeing The Light 30

The Well Wisher 33

Good Manners 34

The Bond Of Sorrow 35

Seeing's Not Believing 37

You Can't Win 'Em All 38

Quick Thinking 39

Good References 40

The One Divine Person 41

Hey, Mr Porter 42

Expensive Fare 43

Memories 44

Brains 45

Unwanted Gift 46

Take Your Pick 47

The Philanthropist 48

The Philosopher 49

Prayer Rewarded 51

The Unknown Soldier 53

The Sacred Cow 54

The Benefit Of The Doubt 55

Good Advice 56
The Good Wife 57
Updated 59
The Last Compliment 61
Danegeld 63
The Hero 64
The Great Let-down 66
The Tipster 67
The Prospector 68
Pride and Prejudice 69
The Gamblers 71
The Miracle 72
The Artist 73
The Fearful Tourist 75
The Contract 77
The Penance 78
The Honest Lecturer 79
A Different View 80
Bargain Hunter 81
Mistaken Identity 82
The Good Samaritans 83
Slow Coach 85
The Historian 86
The Reunion 87
The Family Painting 88
All Forgiven 89
Economics 91
Business As Usual 92
Tactics 93
Hind-Foresight 94
A Relative of the Groom 95
The Phone Call 96
Racial Pride 97
The Economist 98
Blind Love 99
Well, Well 100
Great Expectations 101
Living Out 102
Late Arrival 104

Divine Revenge 105
Blind Faith 106
Chutspa *(a hard neck)* 107
Research Rewarded 108
Not To Worry 109
Progress 110
A Fishy Story 111
Diplomacy 113
Excelsior 115
Ad Infinitum 117
The First Lesson of History 118
Tact 120
The Humble One 121
The Dead Loser 122
Marital Bliss 123
Chanukah Gift 125
Miscellany 126

The Cross Irishman

There was a hold-up in the production of the film. The leading actor refused to carry the cross.

"I am an actor," he exploded, "*not* a stunt man. Get a scene-shifter to carry it."

Despite all pleas he remained adamant – no stand-in, no film. That was final.

After much searching, the director came across Paddy, and after eyeing him up and down he decided he would fit the part. He was a fine stand up of an Irish navvy and was fit to carry any cross; with plenty of make-up he would be a replica of the leading actor.

"Would you like to earn an extra tenner, Paddy?" he asked.

Paddy smacked his lips.

"Ten pounds you said, sir," he replied. "Begorrah, I would indeed, but what's the catch?"

"No catch at all, Paddy," said the director, quickly explaining what had happened and what Paddy would have to do.

"All we want you to do is to walk about forty yards with the cross fixed on your back. Keep your head bowed low with your eyes fixed on the ground. Take no notice of the whips you will be hit with – they are all imitation and won't hurt."

Paddy readily agreed, so the scene was all set, the cameras were turned on, and Paddy started to walk with the cross on his shoulders. The spectators booed and hissed, but Paddy took no notice. Then when he had gone about twenty yards a little Jewish actor stepped forward and spat in his face. This proved too much for Paddy. He immediately dropped the cross and planted a strong right hander on the chin of the actor, who fell unconscious. Pandemonium reigned. Actors, producers et al rushed around Paddy.

"Nobody spits in my face," he shouted, "and gets away with it."

The director at last got him to one side and explained that it was all part of the film.

"According to the Bible it happened to Christ, and, after all, the film must be true to real life," he said.

Paddy agreed, and the whole sequence was once again set in motion. Paddy performed perfectly. He again ignored the boos and the hisses. He reached the spot where the actor, now recovered, again stepped forward, and with an even greater display of hatred, spat right into his face. This time Paddy held on to the cross, but turning to the actor he shouted, "Be Jasus, I'll see you after the Resurrection!"

Gratitude

Grandma was having a lovely time in Miami. The sea was beautifully calm and the sun shone brightly in a temperature of over 100 degrees. The hotel was superb, the cuisine and service impeccable – and they specialised in Jewish food.

But she was not entirely happy. She had heard on the radio that New York was being swept by a blizzard. Snow drifts covered the country surrounding the city and she was very concerned about her grandson, Irving. So she decided to ring her daughter and have the boy flown down to Miami the following morning. He would enjoy the warm sunshine and the golden beaches.

That evening it was all arranged by telephone, and the next day her grandson arrived as planned. Proud as a peacock, Grandma made straight for the beach and, with great pride, showed off the new arrival to all and sundry. That night she felt twenty years younger, and the next morning they were both up early and, after a good breakfast, sauntered down to the beach again.

Little Irving was having a great time and, as Granny sat in a deck-chair watching over his movements, he amused himself by building sand castles by the ocean.

Suddenly tragedy struck – a freak wave swept on to the beach and, on retreating out to sea, swept the child with it. Grandma went hysterical, but being a deeply religious woman she knew that only a miracle could get the boy back.

"Oh, God," she screamed, "do me a favour, please, please, please return my little Irving to me. How can I tell his mother and father that he has been drowned? I'll go to the Schule on the Sabbath; I'll give generously to the Rabbi; I'll support Israel; I'll do anything, only please, please God save my little Irving!"

As if in answer to her prayer, once again the wave swept on to the beach and again retreated quickly out to sea, leaving little Irving sitting on the shore as if nothing had happened. Grandma raced down and clasped him fondly in her arms. Turning her eyes heavenwards, she shouted, "Thank you, God, thank you for saving my grandson.

14

I'll keep all the promises I made.   But tell me, dear God, what became of the twenty dollar sun hat he was wearing?"

Purged

Tom was a wild youth, and his father, who could never understand his boyish enthusiasm, tried to keep him on the straight and narrow. Their arguments became fiercer and fiercer as time went by and, despite the intervention of the lad's mother in the role of peacemaker, Tom decided that he had had enough of living at home and that he would join the Irish Army.

But his visions of a carefree life were soon shattered and he realised that his father's discipline was nothing compared to the rigidity of the Army. In desperation he wrote to his mother and begged her to persuade his father to put up the necessary cash to buy him out of the army at once. His surprise and anger were great when, after a few days, he received a letter from his mother saying that his father had decided to leave him in the army for a few years as it would make a man of him.

Left with no option, Tom served out the five years to which he was committed and returned home a wiser and more sober man as his father had forecast. Army life had showed him the folly of his ways and he soon settled down and became an example of hard work and industry. After a few years his father passed away and Tom inherited a comfortable farming business.

About a year later as he was driving a herd of cattle down the road the parish priest approached in his car and, as is the custom in rural parts of Ireland, stopped to have a chat. Admiring the fine herd that Tom was driving, the priest remarked how well the business was going and what a debt of gratitude Tom owed to his father who, in the priest's opinion, had always been a very honest and hard-working man. Tom agreed completely.

"A great man indeed. I often regret the rows and arguments that we had in the past. I was young and foolish then and knew no better."

"Ah well," the priest replied, "we all did foolish things in our youth but usually make up for it later. The poor man must be a year dead now."

"Aye, he'll be a year dead next Friday. May God have mercy on him," Tom replied.

"Oh well," the priest said, "I'd better arrange a Mass for his dear departed soul."

"No, Father, I want no Mass," Tom said.

The priest looked at him aghast.

"No Mass! *No* Mass! For your poor father's soul! In God's name, *why* not?"

"Well, the way I see it is this," came the reply. "If he's in Heaven, which I hope he is, he doesn't need it. If he's in Hell, it's no good to him."

The priest crossed himself.

"How *dare* you speak about your departed father in such terms. Have you considered that the poor man's soul may be in Purgatory and that a Mass might shorten his time of penance there?"

"I have thought about that all right," Tom said, scratching his head, "and I have decided to leave him there for a few years as it will make a man of him."

An Saoi – Hockum – Man Of Wisdom

It was Saturday night and "Blooms" was packed full of the local Jewish community celebrating the end of the Sabbath. The wine flowed freely and the glasses clinked merrily to the accompaniment of the clatter of diamonds and the swish of mink coats.

Suddenly through the door came two big Irish navvies, complete with picks, shovels, wellington boots and overalls liberally splattered with mud. Everyone stared in amazement. It was unheard of that such attire should be seen in "Blooms". The head waiter rushed into the office where Mr Bloom was seated.

"Mr Bloom," he said, "we got trouble. There are two big Irish navvies in the restaurant waiting to be served. What will I do? Will I tell them to leave?"

But Mr Bloom, as usual, took everything in his stride.

"No, Manny," he said. "We, as Jews, cannot do a thing like that. We, ourselves, have been victimised because of our nationality. So listen, give them the best table in the restaurant, put two waiters attending on them, serve them the best meal you've got and then, at the end, charge them double. They won't come back anymore."

The two navvies appeared to enjoy the meal. When the bill was presented, they did not seem at all surprised. They straight away paid up, gave the waiters a pound each, and then left. The head waiter was greatly relieved. He told Mr Bloom what had happened and Mr Bloom said, "Well, that's that. They won't come back again."

However, when the following Saturday night came round, no less than six navvies arrived and seated themselves at a table. Again the head waiter rushed to Mr Bloom and told him the story.

"There are six of them now," he said. "What are we going to do?"

Mr Bloom thought for a moment.

"Give them the same treatment as last time," he said. "Good service, the best meal you got – but charge them triple. *That* will ensure they will not come back."

But, to the waiter's great surprise, when the bill was presented, the Irishmen paid up smilingly and left five pounds tip. Mr Bloom shook his head when he heard it, convinced that at that price they would not return. However, on the following Saturday night when the festivities were very high, two lorry loads of navvies arrived at the door, gaily barged in and occupied ten tables. This time the head waiter panicked. He dashed into Mr Bloom and said, "Mr Bloom, Mr Bloom, there are about forty Irish navvies out there now. What am I going to do?"

Mr Bloom thought for a while.

"Manny," he said, "let's be sensible. Give them the best service possible. Give them the best meal in the house. Charge them four times the normal amount and get the bleeding Jews out of the place as quick as possible."

The Parting

Paddy and Harry had played together since they were toddlers, but one day when they met, Paddy announced, very sadly, that they could never play together again.

"Never play together again! Why not?"

Paddy was a little hesitant with his reply and tried to break the news gently.

"Well, Harry," he said, "it's because you are Jewish."

But Harry had the answer to that. "Jewish!" he said. "What difference does that make? After all, we are not playing for money."

A Family Affair

Father Murphy arrived at the Golden Gates to the delight of St Patrick.

"Father Murphy," he said, "Father Murphy, we are delighted to have you here. You have been a shining example of all that the Church taught. You built a school and a Church which are living monuments to your dedication and holiness. So, welcome to Heaven, Father. Step inside, *nobody* could be more welcome."

The priest was delighted, but an even greater surprise was to come when St Peter explained that rewards in Heaven were given to suit the tastes of the lucky ones.

"We know that what little leisure time you had in Ireland you spent admiring the countryside, so for your reward here we have a new motor cycle ready; no petrol, no punctures, no tax, no insurance – and you will never have a breakdown or an accident. So you can roam the vast expanse of Heaven to your soul's content and the scenery will change daily."

Father Murphy was delighted and in no time at all he was away for a spin. The gentle breezes of Heaven and the wondrous views were beyond his greatest expectations. Then suddenly in the distance a large Rolls Royce saloon loomed into view. He looked with great respect and awe and then suddenly stopped. It was a beauty – chauffeur-driven, air-conditioned, and with library, television, and swimming pool. Then, to his amazement, he saw that the occupant was Rabbi Cohen – an old friend from Ireland whom he had known for years before he passed to his reward.

At supper that night St Patrick had a word for everybody.

"Well, Father Pat," he said, "and how did your first day in Heaven go off?"

"Very nice," replied the priest, and carried on with his meal.

St Patrick sensed there was something amiss.

"Father Pat," he said, "come on now, what's on your mind? The golden rule here is that a soul must not harbour a grievance, so out with it!"

"Well, all right," agreed the priest, "there *is* one thing that upsets me. As you know, I had thirty thousand Catholics in my parish and I did my absolute best for them. Now Rabbi Cohen had, at most, one hundred Jewish parishioners to see to and, whilst not being uncharitable in the House of God, I must say that he was not any more popular with his flock than I was. Yet his reward is what I can only describe as a heavenly saloon – and *I* got a motor cycle! It doesn't seem right to me."

St Patrick appeared sympathetic.

"Ah, Father Pat," he said, "I know how you feel, but you must try and understand what it is like in this place. Isn't Cohen a relative of the Governor?"

The Grafter

Old Mr Goldsmith believed in hard work and economy and his familiar figure could be seen going to and from his jewellers shop morning and night. He was popular in the district and always had a friendly "hello" and a smile for the people of the street.

One evening, after a hard day's work, as he proceeded homewards he felt a sudden faintness come over him and he collapsed. A good neighbour, seeing what happened, rushed out and put a blanket over him and a pillow under his head, whilst calling to a friend to phone for the ambulance. But the attack was not serious, and after a few minutes Mr Goldsmith opened his eyes. The good neighbour was delighted. "Are you comfortable, Mr Goldsmith?"

The old man shrugged his shoulders.

"I make a living," he said.

Yiddishe Koph

They had to have a parrot. They had seen one in the zoo, and for weeks kept on to their dad to get them one. Eventually he could stand it no longer, so he made his way to his friend Hymie who ran a pet shop down the road.

"Hymie," he said, "do me a favour – I want a parrot."

"Moyshe," Hymie said, "on my life you are lucky! I have got the only Yiddishe-speaking parrot in the world."

"Do me a favour," said Moyshe, "I want no spiel. I just want the parrot."

But Hymie would not let it rest at that. "So you don't believe me," he said. "On my life, should I live that long, this parrot can say the Shama from beginning to end and I'll lay an even fifty to prove it."

Moyshe thought that he was on to a good thing, so he put down his fifty pounds and said, "All right, Hymie, it's a bet."

Hymie turned to the parrot.

"Polly," he said, "say the Shama."

Polly turned her eyes up to Heaven and started *"Shama Oh Israel"* and finished the prayer off completely.

Moyshe thought quickly. He could make a lot of money out of this parrot, so he said, "Hymie, how much?"

"One hundred pounds – but to you seventy-five."

The deal was made and Hymie left with the parrot. On his way home he met his friend Abie.

Abie greeted him affably. "Was machtsdu, Moyshe? What have you got there?"

"Ah," Moyshe replied, "I have something here you have never seen before. Believe it or not, I have the only Yiddishe-speaking Parrot in the world."

Abie laughed.

"Don't tell me," he said, "that you went to Hymie in the pet shop and he fooled you into believing it."

"Well," Moyshe said, "if you are so sure, I'll bet you an even one hundred pounds that this parrot will say the Shama from beginning to end."

"It's a bet," Abie said and put down the money.

Abie turned to the Parrot. "Polly," he said, "say the Shama." But to his utter dismay there was no response. The parrot remained silent. Despite two more appeals the bird refused to speak.

"Zama Gesind, Moyshe," said Abie and walked off laughing with the two hundred pounds.

Moyshe turned in anger to the parrot.

"Polly, you saw that I had an even one hundred pounds bet, why did you not say the Shama?"

The parrot looked at him laughing and shouted, "Do me a favour, you big smo, that fellow will give you ten to one tomorrow."

What's In A Name?

Outside the Schule on Saturday Moyshe met his old friend Hymie whom he had not seen for a number of years.

"Hymie," he said, shaking his head, "how are you? How is the business?"

"The business!" said Hymie, very downhearted. "Don't talk about the dead. On Monday I am going bankrupt."

Moyshe grinned, shook his head and said, "You have made the business over to the wife, of course?"

His friend shook his head.

"No," he said, "I have not."

"To one of the children then?" Moyshe asked.

"No," his friend replied, "not to one of the children either."

Moyshe was more puzzled than ever.

"Well," he said, "do me a favour. You *must* have given the business to somebody. Surely you are not going to declare your full assets?"

Sorrowfully, Hymie replied, "Moyshe, my friend, the truth is that I have nothing to sign over to anybody. I am bankrupt."

Moyshe looked at his friend in amazement and pity.

"Hymie, my dear friend," he said, "you are not bankrupt – you are *broke*!"

Different Tastes

Bridget always had an eye for attractive tea and dinner sets, and she also had a vase or two of flowers in her neat little home in the country at all times.

One day, in Dublin, she decided that she would spend a couple of hours at the National Museum. She gazed with envy at the beautiful pieces of china there. Suddenly a Ming vase caught her eye and she stared at it in admiration. She felt a terrible urge to take it in her hands to feel it. When nobody was looking, she lifted the vase up and fondled it gently. This was something she would really like to own.

Just then she saw an attendant approach and she hurriedly tried to put the vase back. In her haste she dropped it to the ground and it smashed into a thousand pieces.

The curator rushed out, panic stricken; his voice could be heard all over the building as he screamed, "You fool, you fool. Do you realise you have smashed the only Ming vase in the whole museum and that it was over five thousand years old?"

Bridget looked at him sternly.

"You'd think by the row you are kicking up that the end of the world had come," she said. "Thank God it wasn't a new one."

The Home Lover

All his life he had cherished the ambition to visit Israel. After years of saving, the great day arrived, and with much anticipation he boarded the plane and took off on the long flight to the homeland of his ancestors.

He had heard from his parents the strange sounding names of Haifa, Bethlehem, Jerusalem and, of course, he had been told of the traditional visit to the Wailing Wall. That, he had decided, would be the first place he would see. So, on landing, he went straight there.

Placing the backs of his hands against the wall and beating his forehead against the palms, he cried, "I want to be among my people, I want to be among my people."

A Rabbi praying close by heard his mournful plea. He approached and gently laid his hand on the pilgrim's shoulder, saying, "My son, my son, you *are* amongst your people."

But Hymie refused to be comforted.

"No, no," he cried. "My people are all on the beaches in the South of France."

The Hod Carrier

Paddy arrived from Ireland full of youthful enthusiasm and muscle. After a short while, he found a job on the building as a hod carrier. He found digs locally and, on his return from work on his first day, the landlady asked him, "Well, Paddy, how did you get on? What is the work like?"

Paddy laughed.

"Oh," he said, "there is no work. I just carry up the bricks, give them to the bricklayers, and then *they* do all the work."

Doubting Manny

Manny was a very rich man, but was reaching retirement age. He had one son whom he worshipped and he decided that it was time that the boy took over the business. So he broke the news to the boy and said, "Son, come down then to the factory. I want to show you around and introduce you to the staff. You must carry on when I'm gone."

The boy was delighted and took the greatest interest in all that went on in the factory. When the tour was over and they were outside the front door, the father stopped.

"Son," he said, "do me a favour. Go back inside and go up to the first floor and open the window."

The boy looked at him in amazement, but the father would stand for no argument.

"Go on," he insisted, "do as you are told."

In a few minutes the boy was standing inside the open window.

Manny cupped his hand round his mouth and shouted, "Son, stand on the window-sill."

The boy carried out his father's instruction and stood perilously poised on the window-sill.

The father held out his arms and shouted, "Come on, son, jump – I will catch you."

The boy stared at his father in disbelief and was about to argue when his father again shouted, "You can trust me. I promise I will catch you and you won't get hurt."

The lad, believing his father, jumped, but, as he did so, Manny stepped back, putting his hands in his pockets, and the boy crashed to the ground. He lay there writhing in agony.

Finally the boy managed to gasp, "Father, do me a favour. What are you trying to do, *kill* me?"

The father laid a gentle hand on his son's shoulder.

"No, son," he said, "not kill you. I was just giving you your first lesson in business. Trust no one – not even your own father."

Seeing the Light

Paddy and Seamus met as they left the Greyhound Track at Kilkenny. Paddy looked on top of the world, but it was apparent from the expression on the face of Seamus that he had not backed a winner all night.

"Had a bad night then?" Paddy asked.

"A bad night indeed!" said Seamus. "Do you know that I have not backed a winner since God knows when? How did you get on?"

Paddy replied, "I always do the same bet – three dogs and three winners. I have not backed a loser for the past six months."

"Be God, you must be well in the know, although I find it hard to believe," said Seamus.

"Believe it or not, it is true," said Paddy, "and what's more I will never back a loser again."

"You are joking, of course," said Seamus, "but, anyhow, good luck to you. I like to see a man winning, but I could do with a winner myself right now."

By this time they had reached the nearest pub.

"Would you like a drink to help you on the way home?" Paddy asked.

"Well, I would," said Seamus, "but I am broke and I will be poor company."

Paddy was in a philanthropic mood. After a couple of hours they were both warmed up, and losses were forgotten.

"It's incredible," said Seamus, "six months without a loser! God, what would I not give for three winners at Clenmel tomorrow night."

"It can be done," said Paddy, "and it's quite easy."

Seamus pressed the point.

"Well, if you have any tips, I would appreciate a hint. To tell you the truth I am on my last legs and, God forgive me, I am even thinking of packing the game in."

"Oh, you mustn't do that," Paddy exclaimed. "Here, I will tell you the secret, but you must swear on your oath that it will never pass your lips."

"I will swear anything you like," said Seamus, "and, what's more, I will keep my word."

"Very well," Paddy said, "I will tell you the secret. Tomorrow morning buy the newspaper and pick any three dogs at any track you like. Then, on the way to the track, go into your local church and say three *Hail Marys*, light three candles, and away you go and back the three dogs. Have as much money as you like on them – they are sure to win."

Seamus, in his present financial state, was prepared to try anything. "But," he asked, "what happens if we should both go to the same track and back three different dogs?"

"You have a point there. I have been considering that," Paddy said, "and to avoid complications we will meet every morning and choose our tracks. Tomorrow night I will go to Dublin and you go to Thurles."

Next morning Seamus bought his paper. He made his three selections and that evening, on the way to the track, he went into the church and said his prayers, lit three candles, and was away. Sure enough, the three dogs won. Beyond himself with delight he could hardly wait for the following morning.

"Paddy," he said, "it's incredible, but it worked. I chose three names at random and they all won at big prices. It may have been a coincidence, but maybe you have something. Where are you going tonight?"

"I am off to Newbridge. You had better go to Shelbourne Park."

After a few drinks they parted company, agreeing to meet the following morning. Sure enough, the three dogs that Seamus picked all won – and at good prices again. As arranged Paddy and Seamus met again next morning to plan the night's excursion.

"I'm going to Harold's Cross," Paddy said. "You had better go to Waterford."

Seamus was by this time getting a little bit greedy.

"Tell me, Paddy," he said, "is there any limit to what we can win?"

"Oh no," Paddy told him, "providing you carry out my instructions you cannot lose."

"Very well," said Seamus, "I will teach the bookies a sharp lesson tonight. I will get my money back with interest."

Next day they met and planned the night's business as usual. But it was apparent from Seamus' expression that all was not well when they met the next morning.

"What's the matter?" Paddy enquired. "You do not look too happy."

"Happy!" said Seamus. "You and your bloody system; I am broke – out of house and home. I went for the scoop last night and the whole three let me down."

Paddy looked at him in amazement.

"Impossible, impossible," he said. "It *can't* be true. There must be some explanation. Are you absolutely sure that you went to the church, said the prayers, and lit the candles?"

"Of course I did," replied Seamus.

Paddy, however, pressed the point.

"Are you *absolutely* sure, because now I am worried myself."

"One-hundred-percent certain," Seamus insisted. "In fact I remember that after I had finished the prayers and put the donation in the box I found that the candle container was empty. However, I remember thinking at the time that the box at the other side of the church might be full so I lit the three candles one after the other. In actual fact I remember thinking how very big they were compared with the candles I had lit on the other nights. They were about three inches thick and two feet high."

Paddy's face reddened in anger. He grabbed his friend by the neck and shouted, "Seamus, you bloody idiot. Sure the big candles are for the horses!"

The Well Wisher

The Rabbi answered the door in response to a loud knock.

Standing there, the caller, complete with Bible in hand, said, "I am a Jehovah's Witness."

"Muzzletov!" replied the Rabbi. "I hope you win your case."

Good Manners

Little Jimmy had been invited to his first birthday party and his mother, fearful for his good manners, had spent a few days lecturing him on how to behave himself.

"When you are offered sweets," she said, "*only* take one. Don't appear to be greedy and don't eat more than anybody else."

There were lots of little boys and girls at the party and many of them did not seem to have the sense of manners that had been instilled into little Jimmy. Towards evening the goodies were beginning to get scarce and Jimmy's appetite was still not satisfied. Then the little boy whose birthday it was approached him with a tray, on which were two apples.

One of the apples was a beautiful, shiny, red, very large one and the other an undersized, unappetising-looking fruit.

"Would you like an apple, Jimmy?" the little boy said. "There are only two left, one each – take one."

"Oh, thank you very much, Paddy," replied Jimmy. "You take one. You have your first pick."

But Paddy had obviously also been lectured in good manners and he insisted on Jimmy having the first choice. Eventually after a lot of argument Jimmy decided that he would take his pick first, and he took the large apple. Paddy was quite upset and said so.

"That is very bad manners, Jimmy," he said. "You should have taken the *small* one."

"Tell me, Paddy," Jimmy said, "if it had been your choice, which one would you have taken?"

"I would have taken the smaller one, of course."

Jimmy smiled at him.

"So why argue?" he said. "You *have* got the small one."

The Bond of Sorrow

Hymie was a widower. His wife died when his only son, Manny, was just a toddler. However, the kid wanted for very little, and the father devoted his complete life to his son's welfare. The boy himself was a good, studious and grateful son. In fact in all the examinations he came first. And Hymie took great pride in relating his son's brilliance to all his friends at the Schule.

Time passed by and the great day came when Manny was taking his finals at Cambridge. Sure enough, once again he was first in the class. Hymie planned a great welcome home for his son, and out of his secret savings he had a beautiful sports car awaiting his son when he arrived.

"Manny, my dear boy," Hymie said, "I am very proud of you. All my work, all my hopes have now been justified."

The boy, too, expressed his great appreciation of all his father's efforts.

"Dad," he said, "if it weren't for you, I would never have been anything but a tailor. You gave up your pleasures, you worked seven days a week to put me through college, and, believe me, there is no one who appreciates it more than me. But now, Dad, there is one thing that I must tell you. I know that it may come as a great shock to you, but please try to understand that I have given it very great consideration and I have absolutely made up my mind."

He paused for a while and then looked straight at his father and said, "I am becoming a Roman Catholic."

The father stood speechless. He saw all his years of toil, worry and struggle flash away in one terrible second. He would be the laughing stock of the whole Schule. How could he tell the Rabbi? So he pleaded and pleaded and quoted the Scripture to his son to make him change his mind, but the boy was adamant. In desperation he rushed out of the house and went to the Schule, and there he fervently beseeched the Lord God to intervene and guide his son's destiny from this terrible end.

After a while a shadow appeared over the Torah. Hymie gazed in amazement. There, standing in front of him was the Lord God Himself.

"Hymie," He said, "Hymie, you got trouble?"

"Trouble? Trouble?" Hymie sighed, "My God, have *I* got trouble? My son, my only son, is becoming a Catholic."

The Lord approached Hymie with compassion on his face and tears in his eyes. He laid a gentle hand on Hymie's shoulder.

"Hymie, my dear landsman, I know *exactly* how you feel. My own lad did the same thing!"

Seeing's not Believing

The father and young son were strolling along on a farm by a hedgerow in summer bloom. Suddenly the little boy noticed some red berries beginning to burst out on all the broad trees. All excited, he shouted, "Dad, Dad, what are they?"

The father looked.

"Michaeleen, alanna, them are blackberries."

But the little boy would not be fobbed off with that answer.

"But, Dad," he said, "they can't be blackberries because they are red."

But the father knew his countryside.

"That's right, son, they are blackberries alright. But when they are red, that means they are green."

You Can't Win 'Em All

Paddy had a runner in the last race – well drawn, fit as a fiddle, with lots of exercise and good food. He was confident of his dog scoring an easy victory. He kept well away from the crowd, fearing that if any of his friends asked him what the dog's chances were he would have to tell them a lie. If not, they would all have a wager on him and so the betting odds would be greatly reduced.

His trick, however, was not to prove one hundred per cent successful, and Mike, his friend, spied him out in the distance. Quickly he bounded over to Paddy.

"I am in dead trouble, Paddy," he said. "I haven't backed a winner all night. Tell me the honest truth, do you think your dog will win the last race?"

The appeal touched Paddy's heart. What size of a bet Mike could afford would not greatly affect the starting price, and Paddy believed that he could keep a secret. Besides, he was an old friend and Paddy liked him.

"Mike," he said, "I am putting you on your word of honour not to repeat what I am going to tell you. I think the dog has a great chance and should win easily."

Mike's face swelled up in anger.

"Paddy," he shouted, "I would have expected better from you. You are telling me that the dog will win easily so that I'll think he is sure to lose, but I happen to know that you really *do* think he will win, so *why* lie to me?"

Quick Thinking

Mr Freedman was locking up after a busy day when a vagrant approached and asked, "Can I have ten pence for a bed, sir?"

"Take it round to the shop in the morning and I'll have a look at it," Mr Freedman answered.

Good References

Mick considered that he would be the ideal applicant for the job. AN HONEST, HARD WORKING, SOBER YOUNG MAN OF IMPECCABLE CHARACTER NEEDED AS CASHIER IN A BUSY SUPERMARKET. That was the position advertised, so he applied immediately. Within a few days he was called for interview and, after giving full particulars of his education and family background, the interviewer asked him for the usual reference.

"Well," Mick said, "I have not previously been employed. However, if you would write to the following they will vouch for me: The Governor, Mountjoy Gaol; The Chief Probation Officer, Dublin City; The Chief Inspector, Dublin Fraud Squad; and The Secretary of Alcoholics Anonymous."

The interviewer's face fell and he told Mick not to contact them, but they would ring him. Mick thanked him sincerely and left with a smile on his face.

The following week Mick received a letter asking him to come for a further interview, and on entering the interviewing room he was addressed angrily.

"Young man, why did you waste my time asking me to write to those people for references. They have all replied saying that they have never heard of you."

Mick looked him squarely in the eye.

"Then tell me, sir, what better references can you have?"

The One Divine Person

It was going to be the biggest day in his life. A day of joy and happiness in entering into a new spiritual world. Young Paddy took it all very seriously. Sunday was his big day – his first Holy Communion. Saturday was his first Confession, and all through the night before, he examined his conscience in great detail. Next day he joyfully entered the confessional box and reverently bent down to tell what little sins he had committed to the priest. On leaving the confessional box, his parents, waiting in the church, noticed that the usual expression of joy and happiness was not on his face.

Young Paddy knelt down in the pew and his parents waited while he said his penance. They waited and waited, and after a couple of hours decided that he should have finished his penance by then.

His mother approached him and said, "Come on home, Paddy. You don't have to spend all day praying."

But the child refused to move. His mother insisted.

"Come on home, come on home."

But the child still refused.

"I can't go yet, Mother. I have to think."

His mother went back to her seat and waited for a few minutes before approaching Paddy again.

"Come on, come on, Paddy, or we'll go without you."

Again the child refused to budge.

"No, not yet, Mother. I am thinking."

"Well," said his mother, "you can think at home. Come on home now."

"But," said the child, "I am supposed to say my penance before I leave the church."

"Well," said his mother, "it is over two hours since you left the confessional. What terrible penance did you get, or did you commit murder or something?"

"No, Mother," young Paddy replied. "The priest told me to say three *Hail Marys* and I only know one!"

42

Hey, Mr Porter

The American was visiting the birthplace of his parents and, having travelled from the West Coast, was very tired. So he decided, on boarding the train in Dublin, that, in spite of all his good intentions, he would ignore the beauty of the Irish countryside and sleep until he arrived at the small station of Milford.

He called the guard and explained the position.

"Man," he said, "I sure am tired. For twenty-four hours I haven't closed an eye. So when the train reaches Milford I expect to be sound asleep. Here is five dollars and make darn sure you wake me when we get there."

Sure enough, as soon as he was seated in the carriage he dozed off and slept soundly throughout the journey. On awakening, he found that he was in Cork City, and from his meagre knowledge of Irish geography he realised that he had passed his station by at least a hundred miles. Blazing with anger, he sought out the guard and demanded an explanation.

"Paddy," he shouted, "what the goddamn kind of a hobo are you? I gave you five dollars and told you that I was to be let off at Milford, and *that* is a hundred miles back up track."

The guard looked at him in amazement. Scratching his head, he said, "I can understand you being very angry, sir, but I am sure the fellow I threw off at Milford is twice as mad. After all, he gave me ten dollars to wake him up when the train got to Cork."

Expensive Fare

The names of the places he had learnt in his New Testament at school in Ireland had always intrigued Peadar, and throughout his life names like Bethlehem, Nazareth and the Mount of Olives were places he had longed and longed to see. To walk the Way of the Cross to Calvary, to see where Christ walked upon the waters – these were his cherished dreams.

And then fate took a hand when one day he won a five hundred pounds prize in a raffle. Delighted, he set off for Israel and saw with wonder the places he had read and dreamed about. However, he left what he considered to be the most alluring place – where Christ walked upon the waters – until the day of his departure.

He stood in solemn thought by the sea but was interrupted by an Israeli who approached him.

"Would you like a boat trip on the waters?" he enquired. The very idea delighted Peadar.

"I would indeed," he replied.

But, as money was beginning to run short, he asked, "How much would it cost?"

"One hundred pounds," came the reply.

Peadar looked at him in astonishment.

"One hundred pounds! What boat have you got, the *Queen Elizabeth*?"

But the Israeli did not see it from that point of view.

"It's not the boat that matters," he said. "Do you realise that I will row you over the very waters where Jesus Christ Himself walked nearly two thousand years ago?"

But Peadar didn't agree with his point of view either.

"Well, at a hundred pounds a time I wouldn't blame Him for walking," he said.

Memories

It was the custom at a funeral in a certain diocese in Ireland that when the burial ceremony was completed by the priest, one of the mourners who had known the deceased person would come forward and say a few words to the honour of his late friend.

But when old Pat was buried, the small number of mourners present all remained silent. The priest looked around and waited a little while, then he said, "Old Pat has been in the parish since he was born nigh eighty years ago. Surely some of you who have known him most of his life would like to come up and pay him a last tribute."

This appeal evoked no response and silence reigned. Suddenly out of the group a voice said, "His brother was even worse."

Brains

The new intake of pupils was being graded by the headmaster and he was very impressed by young Mick's success in geography.

"Mick," he said, "I am delighted with your results from your previous school. I notice that for the past four years you have been top of your class in geography. It would appear to be your strongest subject. Now tell me, young man," he continued, "can you prove that the world is round?"

Mick looked up, his eyes wide with amazement, and replied, "I never said it was."

Unwanted Gift

The Golden Anniversary was fast approaching, and although anniversaries were never celebrated in the marriage, the children felt that as this was such an important occasion their mother must receive a very special present. Only after long arguments did the father at last agree and one day on the way home from the synagogue he raised the subject with his wife.

Naturally she was delighted with the thought, but, despite all his suggestions, he found her very hard to please. In desperation he said, "Choose your own anniversary gift."

"Well," she said, "I often sit by the window and think how wonderful it would be if when the time comes I could be buried in the little plot at the end of the cemetery overlooking Sydney's house. I feel that I could look down on him and my grandchildren, and even though it's a foolish idea the thought of it makes me happy."

It was agreed, and the next day the plot was duly allocated to her for occupation some time in the future.

Quickly another year passed and her expectations of another present were running high, but the great day brought no response. Her disappointment showed in her face, and although he was used to feminine moods this one proved too much for the husband. After supper he could stand the strain no longer.

"Since morning," he said, "you've had a long face; you have not spoken two civil words all day long. What's the matter? What have I done wrong?"

"Don't you know what day it is? Don't you know it's our fifty-first anniversary and you haven't even mentioned a present?" she complained.

"Present! Present! Do me a favour. I gave you an expensive present last year and you haven't used it yet."

Take Your Pick

Making a choice between two options had always been the curse of his life. Somehow, Paddy had always picked the wrong one. He could have gone to Dublin University or Trinity College. He picked the latter, and all his life regretted it. He had a choice of studying for the priesthood or accountancy. He picked the latter and again regretted it. He had fallen in love with two sweethearts and for years lived in fear of making the wrong choice – he did!

A business venture demanded that he should fly to America, so he rang up the booking office for a flight.

"Certainly, sir," the clerk said, "we have vacant seats on Aer Lingus and on Pan-Am. Which would you prefer to travel on?"

Once again Paddy was bedevilled by making a choice. However, he was not worried about flying and said quickly, "Aer Lingus."

On the appointed day he took off from Dublin Airport, but when the plane was about halfway across the Atlantic the captain's voice came over the intercom.

"Ladies and gentlemen," he said, "the plane has developed serious engine trouble. Would you please read carefully the instructions to be followed in case of an emergency as we may have to make a crash landing on arrival."

Everybody paled with fear, but Paddy showed no signs of apprehension. Turning his eyes up to heaven, he shouted, "St Francis, save me."

Back came the reply, "Which St Francis do you mean – St Francis Xaviour or St Francis of Assisi?"

The Philanthropist

Simon's luck turned at last. After years spent in buying tickets, entering draws and competitions he had won one hundred thousand pounds in the Irish Sweep. Regretting the years when he could not afford to give his beloved wife the things he wished for her, he now decided that he would more than make up for the lean years.

Putting his arm gently on her shoulder, he said, "Now, my dear Rachel, you can have all you ever wished for in life – that fur coat you always looked at when you passed the shop window; a nice little car with a chauffeur to drive you around; the little cottage in the country which you always dreamed about; and all the things which you so much wanted and to which you were entitled for giving me all the happiness during our married life."

Rachel's face beamed with delight, but then a thought flashed across her mind and she glanced towards the table which was piled high with letters.

"Oh, Simon, Simon," she said, "thanks a million, but what about the begging letters?"

Simon's expression immediately changed. His hand quickly left her shoulder and, wagging a finger in front of her face, he shouted, "Keep sending them, keep sending them."

The Philosopher

Paddy was studying philosophy at Dublin University, and daily he heard reports of an old man down the country who had a fantastic philosophical outlook on life. This old man exercised a great influence over the local community and had the happy knack of settling all disputes and arguments. The young scholar decided that he must see this philosopher, and so he wrote and asked if he might visit him one day. The old man made him welcome, and as the young man arrived at the philosopher's country cottage the old man greeted him and said, "You are in luck, my boy. I have a married couple coming to see me today. Their marriage has completely broken down and they are on the point of parting.

Soon the wife of the failing marriage arrived. Young Paddy sat in an adjoining room and listened. The old man started the proceedings.

"Come, my good woman," he said, "let's get started. Tell me your side of the story."

The woman seemed to relish the opportunity. For a good hour she vilified her husband. She described how he had left her short of money, how he had come home drunk regularly and beaten her up, and on the whole was a despicable type of person.

The old man was very sympathetic. He placed a gentle hand on her shoulder and said, "You poor woman, I agree with you completely."

The wife left, relieved and delighted, and after a short while the husband arrived. The young man listened attentively, wondering what argument the old man would have ready, as he had agreed so completely with the wife's version.

"Now, my good man," he said. "Tell me your side of the story." The husband poured forth a torrent of allegations against his wife. She squandered money, she would not cook his meals, she neglected himself and the children, and in general was a disgrace as a wife.

The old philosopher shook his head in sympathy.

"You poor man," he said, "I agree with you completely."

The husband left, relieved and delighted that someone had believed him, and the old man called out to the student, "Well, son, what did you think of that?"

"I'm sorry," the boy said, "I just do not understand it. The two of them told you completely opposite stories and yet you agreed with both of them. Surely one was right and the other was wrong?"

The old man looked at the boy.

"Son," he said, "I agree with you completely."

Prayer Rewarded

Paddy had been to the market and sold the pig. Then he had met with a friend or two and had gone off to quench his thirst in the local pub. One drink followed another, and then at about six o'clock Paddy realised that all he had left from the price of the pig was one pound. The shock of facing his nagging wife with no money hit him, and he thought long and hard about how he would get his money back. Then he had a brilliant idea. On the way home he would go into the dog track and chance his luck with the remaining pound.

Once inside, he studied the programme very thoroughly but could see nothing to help him recoup his losses, except maybe in the last race which was a hurdle race with five dogs as against six in the normal flat races. The one he took to win and which he backed was twenty to one – a complete outsider with no chance whatsoever. Paddy decided that the interventions of the heavens might be a little helpful, and so, as the dogs were placed in the traps and the hare started on its round, Paddy's voice could be heard above the crowd. "Sacred Heart of Jasus, give the fifth dog a fast break."

Sure enough, when the traps rose, the fifth dog flashed out, leaving the other four flat-footed. As he approached the first hurdle Paddy again resorted to prayer.

"Jasus, Mary and Joseph, get him over the first hurdle safely."

The dog jumped beautifully. However, the first and second favourites collided on the hurdle and crashed. They were now out of the race, so things were beginning to look up.

As the dog approached the second hurdle, Paddy's voice could again be heard beseeching the heavens for a safe jump. Again the dog jumped beautifully, but one of the two remaining runners behind him crashed into the hurdles and fell. It was now a two-dog race with one more hurdle to jump. However, the second dog was making up ground, and the nearer he approached the leader the louder Paddy's voice could be heard.

"Sacred Heart of Jasus and all the Saints in Heaven," he cried, "get him over the last obstacle safely."

As with the other hurdles, the dog jumped beautifully and the other dog crashed into the hurdle and fell.

From the last hurdle to the winning post was a distance of about twenty yards, so there was now no danger to Paddy's twenty pounds. Realising that his dog could now not be beaten because all the others had fallen, Paddy threw his hat up into the sky and shouted, "Now go on, you so and so! You're on your own!"

The Unknown Soldier

It was a State occasion in Israel. One of the world's great presidents was visiting, and all pomp and ceremony had been prepared to do him honour. But, unlike most countries, Israel does not have a tomb of the Unknown Soldier. However, on such a formal occasion a visit to the tomb had to take place. So, conveniently, the fact that no such tomb existed was forgotten and the visit was prepared.

The President approached the grave with great dignity and respect. He bent down to place the customary wreath, and as he did so he saw to his amazement and disgust that on the tombstone was written –

MANNY COHEN, INTERNATIONAL BANKER

The President stepped back and beckoned the accompanying Jewish official towards him.

"What is this?" he said. "I am supposed to be paying tribute at the tomb of the Unknown Soldier. This Manny Cohen was an internationally known world-renowned banker."

The official shrugged his shoulders.

"I agree with you, Mr President," he said. "As a banker everyone in the world knew him, but as a soldier he is completely unknown."

The Sacred Cow

The prize cow was the pride of the farmyard, and now that her time was fast approaching to be delivered of a calf Farmer Murphy was all excitement.

"Paddy," he said to his farm worker, "watch her night and day for the remaining weeks, and no matter where I am or what I'm doing call me immediately she goes into labour."

Paddy, equally anxious as his boss, readily agreed.

"Sir," he said, "whether you are under or over the ground, I'll call you at the first signs."

Tirelessly Paddy kept his vigil, and on Christmas Eve he noticed the big event was at hand. He dashed back to the farmhouse, only to be told by the maid that Mr Murphy had gone to Midnight Mass in the village. He immediately grabbed his bicycle and in a few minutes arrived at the church door. Approaching, he noticed the Sacristan standing there.

"Sorry, Paddy," the Sacristan said, "admission by ticket only."

As quickly as possible Paddy explained the position – all he wanted was to walk up the aisle to where Mr Murphy always sat and he would come out immediately. But the Sacristan was adamant.

"Sorry, Paddy," he said, "if I let you in, I will have to let all the late-comers in, and besides, the service is underway and you will disturb the priest and the congregation, especially with the boots you are wearing."

Paddy was equally adamant.

"I hate to have to kick up a row at the House of God," he said, "but if I am driven to it, I will! After all, I won't be inside a minute until I'm out again, and it's worth more than my job if the calf dies."

The Sacristan, fearing an unholy row, reluctantly agreed to let him in.

"Paddy," he said, raising his clenched fist to Paddy's face, "I'll let you in this time, but if I catch you as much as attempting to say one prayer I'll kill you dead on the way out."

The Benefit of the Doubt

A crowd of Irish navvies were laying cables in a London street. It happened that close by was a house of ill repute.

Early in the morning the Protestant vicar came down the street. He paused for a moment opposite the house, looked up and down the street, then knocked at the door. He was admitted by a lady. The navvies could not refrain from comment.

"The Protestants are all the same," they said, "a bunch of hypocrites – and that fellow, a vicar, is supposed to show good example."

About half an hour after the vicar had left, whom should they see coming down the street but the local Rabbi. He, too, stopped at the house. He looked up and down the street, knocked at the door and was admitted by the same lady. The navvies could not believe their eyes.

"Good God," they said, "fancy the Rabbi going into that house. They are all the same. Thank God we are Catholics, the rest are only a bunch of hypocrites."

After dinner, when work was resumed, to their utter amazement they saw their parish priest coming in the direction of the same house. They stood and looked in astonishment. They were stunned when the parish priest stopped at the house, knocked on the door, and was once again admitted by the young girl. A strange silence fell on the group and then Paddy thought he had found the solution.

"Ah, Jasus, lads," he said, "there must be somebody sick in there."

Good Advice

Paddy loved music and, seeing a Beethoven concert advertised for the Abbey Theatre in Dublin, he decided he would make the long trip to town.

On arriving at the entrance to the city he found that he was lost. He had never been to the Abbey before, so he stopped and said to a pedestrian, "How do I get to the Abbey Theatre?"

The man looked at him pityingly and replied, "Keep practising, son, keep practising."

The Good Wife

It was a busy day in the shop and Sammy was glad when closing time came. He counted the day's takings and locked them safely away. Putting on his leather coat and locking his front door, he sat in his Rover and prepared to drive home through the bitter winter's evening.

Just then a regular customer of his, a beautiful young girl, walked past. As a matter of courtesy and business he called out to her, "If you are going my way, can I give you a lift?"

She was going his way alright and gladly accepted the offer. After about a mile she said, "I live in a flat just on the left, so if you pull up at the next traffic lights it will be fine."

As she alighted, the snow was falling heavily, and in appreciation of his kindness she invited him in for coffee. Sammy protested that his wife would be expecting him and that he must be on his way, but she insisted.

"It will only take five minutes," she said.

Well, she was a good customer and he couldn't be rude, so he switched off the engine and went in with her. She took his coat and seated him on the settee in the sitting-room, saying that she would pop into the kitchen and prepare the coffee. She returned in about five minutes and to his amazement he noticed that she was dressed in a negligée and carrying a tray of coffee and a bottle of brandy.

"It's cold in here," she said. "We'll have a brandy or two first."

A lot of coffee and a lot of brandy was drunk, and a lot of things happened before, looking at his watch, he realised that the time was eleven thirty. In disgust, he jumped up, grabbed his coat and left.

'My God, what have I done?' he thought.

During the rest of the journey home he was full of remorse. He tried to think of all the credible excuses his wife might accept but, try as he would, he could think of nothing which he thought she would believe. He consoled himself with the thought that he had always been a good husband and father, and that, knowing the wonderful relationship which he had with his wife, she would forgive him the one slip in their twenty years of marriage. He decided to tell the truth. As he opened the front door his wife screamed at him, "Where the hell have you been until this hour of the night? I kept the kids up until eleven o'clock and they went to bed crying. The candles are burned out and the fish is completely overcooked."

"Connie," he said, "sit down. I have something terrible to tell you, and you must try in your heart to forgive me."

So, starting from the time he locked the shop door and until he left the temptress's flat, he told her the full sordid story as it happened. When he had finished, the expected torrent of abuse was not directed at him.

"Well," he said, "are you going to forgive me or do you want a divorce?"

"Going to forgive you – want a divorce?!" screamed his wife. "Now tell me the truth. *Who* did you go dog-racing with?"

Updated

The parents were very devout believers and on all occasions adhered strictly to the Jewish faith, and, as their boy was reaching school age, they spent many hours discussing which school he should attend.

Eventually they settled on a very orthodox one and the father proudly took the boy along on his first day.

When he got home that evening from the business, the proud parent queried his boy regarding what he had been taught on his first day at school.

"Papa," his son said, "it was most interesting. We were taught the story of how the Jews returned to the Holy Land."

The father was very interested.

"Tell me about it, son."

"Well," the boy began, "General Moses had advanced way off into Egypt, and suddenly the Egyptian army counter attacked. They sent in wave after wave of dive-bombers to attack the Israeli positions, but the Israelis had by then perfected the ground-to-air missile and shot them down like flies. Then the Egyptians sent in their heavy armour, tanks weighing up to two hundred tons and rocket launchers, but again the Israelis had perfected the armour-piercing bullet and knocked them out as they came.

"Looking on from his helicopter, General Moses realised that he was now too far from his base to contain the reserves that the Egyptians would bring, so he ordered a retreat back into Israel.

"The Israeli engineers mined the land on either side of the retreat and, with their rapid advancing personnel carriers, the Israeli army were within sight of the Red Sea within a few hours, in spite of everything the Egyptians could throw at them. But even the Red Sea, Dad, was no obstacle to them, as General Moses ordered a pontoon bridge to be thrown over it and the army was safely across within a few minutes. Then the Egyptian army proceeded across the bridge, but as they were crossing it in great numbers the Israeli experts exploded an atom bomb which they had cunningly concealed in the bridge and destroyed the bulk of the invading army while the remaining few retreated in disarray."

The father looked in utter disbelief and amazement.

"Tell me, son, did they really *teach* you that in school today?"

Sadness appeared in the little boy's eyes.

"No, Dad," he said, "but if I told you the story they did tell me, you just would not believe it."

The Last Compliment

In the remote country village the parish priest was out on his own in the popularity stakes. A proper Father O'Flynn, and the rich and poor held him in the highest esteem. He had been in the parish for as long as the oldest inhabitant could remember. The young ones had kindly memories of their initiation into the church from his gentle hands, and the parents remembered with happiness that he was the life and soul of the party at their wedding reception.

Then, alas, as with us all, old age inevitably began to take its toll, and one day, not feeling on top of the world, he decided to visit the village doctor for a check-up. After a thorough examination he was advised that the years of hard work were beginning to have their effect on him and that in future he would have to take it much easier.

"Go away to a better climate for the winter months," the doctor said, "and after a spell in a nice comfortable rest home you may come back to us hale and hearty."

When the news leaked out, there was sorrow in the parish. The place won't be the same without him; God speed him back to us, was the general prayer.

During the three months abroad he did not lose touch with his beloved parishioners, and at Mass on Sunday a letter from him was usually read out. In character with his personality his letters were cheerful and full of hope for the future. Then the great day arrived; the curate announced that Father Pat would be coming home again on Wednesday. The street was thronged with people cheering his welcome return.

"Father Pat is tired out after his long journey," the doctor announced, "so please leave him to have a good night's sleep and he will see you all on Sunday."

The crowd dispersed but, alas, the doctor's words did not come true, for next morning at Mass it was announced that their beloved priest had passed to his eternal reward during the night. The excitement of returning and the journey had proved too much for the tired out frame.

The grief of the parishioners was boundless and from all over the parish they came to pay their last respects at his wake. The most affected of all was Mrs. Murphy. She was the town's oldest inhabitant, and as she left the parochial house she had to be consoled by the curate.

"Father O'Brien," she sobbed, "it is sad and weary I am today. I remember the day he said his first Mass in the parish and the day he married me and christened all me children. Many a pound note he slipped me when they were small – and after all that to see him lying there dead. But thank God there is a look of happiness in his holy face. Jasus, he looks grand; them few months abroad done him the world of good!"

Danegeld

The late news on the radio always gave the latest Stock Exchange results and, being heavily involved, Moyshe listened in attentively each night. Seated in his armchair in front of a comfortable fire, he would count his profits or losses for the day and then retire to bed.

One night his calculations were upset by a brick coming hurtling through his window and landing at his feet. He looked at it in horror and amazement, and then noticed that there was a note tied to it. Hurriedly, he tore it open and read:

> *If you do not put twenty thousand pounds in cash in the telephone box at the top of the street by ten o'clock tomorrow night, we will kidnap your wife.*
>
> *Signed 'The Kidnappers'*

Calmly he reclined back in his armchair and re-read the letter then went over to his bureau and returned with a sheet of notepaper and an envelope. Carefully and plainly he wrote his reply:

> *Dear Kidnappers,*
> *On my life I have not got twenty thousand pounds, but please, please keep in touch as I am very interested in your proposition.*

He then walked to the telephone box.

The Hero

He arrived at the Golden Gates of Heaven and knocked for admission.

"Who is there?" St Peter asked.

"It is me," came the reply in a Northern Ireland dialect. "William Churchill Smith, from Sandy Row, Belfast, N. Ireland."

"We don't get many from there," St Peter said and opened the gates.

"I'm afraid," he continued, "accommodation is rather scarce here at the moment. Of course, we are building several new mansions, but meanwhile admission is strictly limited. In fact the only souls we are allowing in are those who have performed deeds of great renown on the earth – feats of bravery, love of your fellow men and such things that prove a man to be of great calibre and character."

"Well," replied William, "surely I must come under that heading."

St Peter shook his head.

"William," he said, "perhaps you may have given a penny to a poor man or something trivial like that, but that is not sufficient to admit you at the present time."

William's face glowered with anger.

"With all due respect," he replied, "I consider that I performed feats of bravery which will be told to the Protestant children of the Holy North while Ireland is divided – and that will be forever."

St Peter looked at him in amazement.

"I am sorry, William," he said, "but as far as I am concerned there have been no feats worth talking about in Ireland since St Patrick banished the snakes."

"Ah, well," replied William with great indignation, "let me tell you something. I myself wooed a devout Catholic girl and brought her into the Holy Orange Order – and even better than that, the morning of our wedding I walked down Anderstown, the thickest Catholic area in Northern Ireland, with me sash across me shoulder and an Orange banner over me head with the words *To Hell with the Pope* written boldly across it."

St Peter looked at him in amazement.

"Well, William," he said, "I can't say I entirely agree with your actions, but I must admit that it called for a lot of determination and character. Excuse me now for a moment while I check your story in the records."

In a short while he re-appeared.

"William," he said, "we have no record of anything like that ever happening; perhaps there may be a page missing. Can you give me any idea of the date it happened?"

"A date!" said William. "It all happened half a minute ago."

The Great Let-down

After months of mock parachute training, Mick and Paddy were ready for their first real jump from an aeroplane.

Having dealt with 'first timers' for a number of years, the instructor was kindness itself.

"Now, lads," he said, "there's nothing to worry about. Get ready to jump when I give the command. After you leave the plane, count to ten and pull the cord on the right-hand side. Your parachute will open and you will float gently down to the ground where the staff car will be waiting to take you back to the mess for the traditional 'first jump' celebration. If by any chance the parachute fails to open, pull the cord on the left-hand side and everything will be all right. Good luck to you. Ready – steady – jump!"

Bravely the two lads jumped out into space and counted carefully up to ten. Mick's parachute did not respond, so, quickly, he pulled the left-hand cord. Again nothing happened.

Looking across at Paddy, he shouted in anger at the top of his voice, "And I bet the bloody car won't be there either."

The Tipster

"How's your luck?" Mick asked his friend Mark as they left the dog track.

"Luck?" Mark replied, "I don't need luck anymore – I've backed twelve winners in a row."

"It's hard to believe," Mick commented. "What's the secret?"

"There is no secret attached to it," Mark replied, "but there is a new feature in the *Jewish Chronicle* which gives a nap selection weekly and the first twelve are all winners. I've backed every one of them. So do yourself a favour, get the *Chronicle* and the selection is on the back."

Mick was first in the newsagent's the following week and, confident that the tipster's advice was better than his own, he went to the track that night. He backed his week's wages on the chosen greyhound. Alas, all good things must come to an end, and the unfortunate dog finished stone cold last.

The following week he met his friend and told him the sad story.

Mark was very sympathetic.

"Yes," he said, I lost a few bob on it myself. However, let's see what he tips this week."

Sure enough, on the back page the nap selection again appeared, but underneath was written: *Sorry that my thirteenth nap let you down but, on my life, I fancied the winner.*

The Prospector

Sammy had spent all his life prospecting for gold in Alaska but unfortunately had never struck it rich. His determination kept him going, and throughout the whole year he never slackened his efforts. His little log cabin was stocked with the usual provisions of a gold miner, and when supplies ran low he would make the long trek to the town and re-stock.

However, one day when it became necessary to make the journey the winter snows had started to fall and, in the hope that one day it would be fine enough for him to travel, he used his provisions carefully. But the snow storms got worse and the drifts piled up around his shack and hunger began to take its toll on his strength – and then all the food was eaten up. He grew weaker and weaker, knowing that the inevitable end could not be very far away.

Lying on his bunk one night, he heard the jingle of a sleigh and the barking of dogs, and he felt that this was the end as he must surely be dreaming. Suddenly there was a great banging on the door and a voice shouted, "Is there anybody in there?"

Weakly he answered, "Who is it, who is there?"

Back came the reply, "We're from the Red Cross."

Sammy seemed to regain all his strength and bellowed, "I've given already!"

Pride and Prejudice

There was great preparation in the Parochial House. The two missionaries were arriving that night for a fortnight's mission in the town. The parish priest was glad that they were coming because he himself could relax for a bit while they were there without feeling any prick of conscience.

He was trying to decide on an appetising meal so he went to a local farmer and got two beautiful fat chickens. His housekeeper cooked them, and as the two missionaries and he sat around the table to eat the deliciously cooked meal, the telephone rang. The housekeeper, however, answered the telephone and called the priest, saying, "You are wanted on the phone, Father."

He rose from the table to answer and came back to apologise to his Jesuit guests that he had an urgent sick call to make. He said, "Please don't wait for me, I may be delayed a little. Carry on with your meal, you must be hungry after your long journey."

Sure enough, he did not return for about two hours, but the thought of that lovely meal awaiting him was a great consolation. However, as he entered the house, the housekeeper said to him, "Father, I'm afraid the chickens have all been eaten. You will have to have fried egg and bacon."

The priest accepted it with humility.

"Never mind, never mind," he said.

When he had finished his meagre helping, the two missionaries and he retired to the sitting-room, and his guests were full of compliments for the wonderful meal.

"Parish Priest," they said, "that was the best meal we have had in years. In fact we are both so full that we feel a short walk before bedtime would help our digestion."

The parish priest agreed and they set off over the country roads. Soon they were passing the house of the farmer who had supplied the two chickens. It was a beautiful summer's evening and the sun was shining brightly. On top of the farmer's gate stood a cockerel – his head held proudly erect, his wings outstretched in the sunlight and his crowing could be heard for miles around. They stopped and the Jesuits admired the bird.

"Ah, what a beautiful bird, but again what a tragedy! There he stands showing off his beautiful plumage and crowing with pride. That is also one of the terrible sins of mankind. Pride to me is a sinful and deadly thing," one of the Jesuits observed.

The other Jesuit nodded his head in agreement, but the parish priest did not agree with their viewpoint.

"Well," he said, "I am not so sure that is true, because without pride there would be very little progress in society and surely the good Lord will allow us to take pride in a notable achievement. Perhaps that bird has something to crow and be proud about. After all, he has two sons in the Jesuits."

The Gamblers

White City stadium had indeed a very small crowd that night, and as they walked to the Underground Pat remarked to Jim, "I suppose the crowd was so small tonight because it's Pasach[1]. There were no Jewish bookies standing and there were very few Jews in the crowd."

Jim agreed with his explanation but not with the cause.

"No," he said, "tonight is not Pasach. Tonight is Yom Kypur[2]."

"Not at all," Pat argued, "Pasach comes before Yom Kypur."

And so the argument continued until they reached the ticket window in the Underground where there happened to be a Jewish punter whom they knew.

"Tell me," asked Pat, "did Pasach or Yom Kypur come first?"

The punter had obviously had a bad night.

"Do me a favour," he said, "I been going to that stadium for ten years and I never saw either of them win a race."

---

[1] The feast of the Passover.
[2] The Day of Atonement.

The Miracle

Brigit had had a lot of trouble and worry in her life, and her religious intuition suggested that she should make a trip to Lourdes. She went and she prayed fervently with the others gathered there. Arriving back at Dublin Airport, she approached the Customs.

"Anything to declare, madam?"

Brigit shook her head. "No, sir, nothing to declare."

"Are you sure, madam?"

"Absolutely sure," Brigit replied.

"Would you mind opening your case, please?" asked the Customs official.

Brigit dutifully opened her case, and from the bottom the official produced a large bottle filled to the top.

"Madam," he queried, "what is this?"

"It is Lourdes holy water," Brigit replied.

But the official was sceptical. He undid the cork, poured a drop onto the tip of his finger and tasted it.

"Madam," he said, "this is gin."

Brigit blessed herself, turned her eyes up to Heaven, and shouted for all to hear, "Holy Jasus, it's another miracle!"

The Artist

He was a very rich man, director of five companies, hardworking and shrewd in business. But then the inevitable take-over bid was made for his companies, and he decided to sell out and live on his capital. When the deal was completed, he sought the advice of his accountant regarding the most profitable way to invest his money.

"Mr Rubenstein," the accountant said, "you are asking me to advise you on a very difficult subject. In these days of rapid inflation, money loses value so quickly. The Stock Market is so uncertain and with money prices rising so rapidly, my advice to you is to buy a very expensive antique. It's something that will increase in value yearly, and you can dispose of it at a profit at any time you wish."

Mr Rubenstein accepted his advice and duly proceeded to a world-famous antique shop in the city. On being approached by an assistant with the usual "Can I help you, sir?" he said, "My name is Rubenstein. I want to buy a Reubens."

"Very well, Mr Rubenstein," the assistant replied. "As it so happens, we have got one for sale. I am afraid it is very expensive. It will cost you three hundred and fifty thousand pounds."

Money was merely being invested, so Mr Rubenstein agreed and the deal was settled.

A year passed by and once again Mr Rubenstein found himself in his accountant's office. The accountant was jubilant.

"You did a very wise thing in buying that Reubens painting. On a rough estimate I would imagine it is worth in the region of four hundred thousand pounds now. I have looked into your affairs very carefully in the last week and would suggest that you now go and buy another antique. I expect the price will increase even more in the next twelve months."

Once again, Mr Rubenstein set off for the antique shop, and by a strange coincidence the very same assistant who had sold him the Reubens approached him. He greeted him warmly and said, "Ah, Mr Rubenstein. Would you care to buy another Reubens?"

His customer looked at him rather sternly and replied, "My name is now Smith. I want to buy a Goya[3]."

---

[3] Jewish slang for Gentile.

The Fearful Tourist

The London tourist was really enjoying his holiday in a leisurely village in Ireland. The pace of life was a revelation after living in London. The rich green of the countryside was in stark contrast to the traffic-filled streets of his native city. Most of all, he was enjoying the evening in an Irish pub where licensing hours seemed to be non-existent, and it was well past daybreak when the party decided to split up.

By this time the Londoner, not being used to Irish whiskey, was finding it difficult to make his legs obey him. On going outside, he was delighted to see a man driving a donkey and cart approaching. Beside the driver sat his faithful dog and in the back of the creel that surrounded the cart, a fat pig. The Londoner gave the sign of thumbing a lift. The donkey and cart came to a halt and the driver enquired, "What's the matter with your thumb, sir?"

"Oh nothing. I notice that you are going towards Murphy's hotel; could you give me a lift?"

The driver readily agreed.

"Sit up on the other side," he said. "It's only about a mile down the road."

When the Londoner had seated himself comfortably, he noticed to his horror that there was a double-barrelled shotgun lying behind him. Now, it is an accepted fact that Englishmen are very sceptical of Irishmen who carry guns, so he politely enquired why this deadly weapon was there.

"Well, you see," the Irishman explained, "it's like this. I come into the market very regularly, and at this time of the morning there is usually a rabbit or a pheasant hopping about the road. So I take a pot shot."

The explanation was accepted with relief. A little further up the road they arrived at a sharp bend, around which a lorry came at high speed and crashed into the donkey and cart.

The tourist was flung into the ditch and he quickly realised that he had probably broken his ribs as well as having his face covered in blood from a severe gash on the forehead. The dog and the pig, however, suffered a worse fate and the dog's two front legs were broken. The animal was screaming in agony whilst the pig's side had been badly torn and there was blood flowing over the road.

The driver, however, escaped serious injury and, quickly surveying the scene and realising that the dog and the pig were beyond redemption, he reached for the shotgun to put them out of their misery and shot them both.

He then turned to the Englishman who was lying moaning in the ditch.

"How are you feeling, sir?" he asked.

Having seen what had happened to the two animals, the tourist quickly replied, "Absolutely bang on, old chap. Never felt better in my life."

The Contract

The local council had advertised for tenders for a small repair job on a footpath. Three replies were received: Murphy quoted £3,000, Smith £6,000, and Cohen £9,000.

As is usual in such cases, the Council Surveyor interviewed the three contractors. Mr Murphy was first in.

"Tell me," the surveyor asked, "how do you break down your quotation of £3,000 for the job?"

"Well," replied Murphy, "I estimate £1,000 for the materials and, as you know, I only employ hard-working Irish tradesmen who do the job on piecework – so I would estimate £1,000 in labour costs. That is a total of £2,000. Add fifty percent to this and there is the £3,000."

Mr Smith was next in. The surveyor said, "We have here an estimate of £6,000 for this job. It is not the lowest and it is not the highest. How do you break it down?"

"Well," Mr Smith replied, "we only use the very best materials, and that would account for £2,000. We only employ specialised highly-qualified tradesmen who take their time and do a very thorough job – that would be another £2,000. That is a total of £4,000. Add fifty percent and there is my estimate of £6,000."

Mr Cohen was last in.

"Tell me, Mr Cohen," asked the surveyor, "how do you break down your estimate of £9,000 for this small job? Murphy has estimated £3,000, Mr Smith £6,000, and your estimate is £9,000. This figure really surprises me. How do you break it down?"

Mr Cohen thought for a moment.

"Well," he said, "there is £3,000 for you, £3,000 for me, and I sub-contract the job to Murphy."

The Penance

He was a stranger in the village, a trampoline artist with the visiting circus, but on Saturday night he went to church to confession. As he knelt before the priest in the confessional he explained that he was a trampoline artist. The priest was not sure what that meant.

"Tell me," he asked, "what is a trampoline artist?"

The stranger did his best to explain.

"Well," he said, "I do body contortions, I do back stretches, I do the splits, I walk on my hands, and somersault in the sky. But, hold on a minute, Father. As you don't know my profession, let me give you a little demonstration."

Quick as a flash he was out before the altar in the church and started his performance. He did his somersaults, did the splits, and walked on his hands with his feet pointing towards the roof.

Part of his act, however, brought an unforeseen happening from Bridie who was kneeling in the confessional queue.

"Excuse me, Mary," she said to her friend. "I have to go home to change my underwear. Father Murphy is giving rough penances tonight."

The Honest Lecturer

Goldfinger and Partner had been established in Dublin for well over fifty years and they ran a very successful business. One day, to their great delight and astonishment, they received an invitation from the Professor of Economics at Dublin University inviting one of them to lecture the students on "How to ran a Successful Business".

Mr Goldfinger gladly accepted the invitation and on the agreed day he stood in front of his young audience.

"Gentlemen," he said, "I am delighted and honoured to be asked to such a brilliant and intellectual audience and I feel inferior to the task. I come from a very humble background and have no qualifications such as you young gentlemen and ladies will one day obtain. As my chauffeur drove me here in my Rolls Royce I kept thinking what on earth I could say that would be of interest to you in the field of business. And then I remembered a little incident which happened last week, and from it I have decided that the most important element in business is – honesty.

"As you all know, with my partner I sell a very good, up-to-date, modern, cheaply priced range of menswear – the best in Dublin in my opinion. In particular, we feature a very good range of hard-wearing men's shirts at almost cost price. Now last week a lady customer came into my shop and picked out for her husband a beautiful shirt selling at under three pounds. I complimented her on her choice, wrapped the shirt up neatly, and gave her the change from a five pound note which she had given in payment. However, as I put the note in the till I noticed that instead of one note there were in fact two stuck together. Now this is where honesty comes into business – should I tell my partner?"

A Different View

They were a grand litter of pups and looked like being real champions. Jack, of course, could not afford to rear the lot of them and he had heard that the local Rabbi sometimes had a little flutter. One day when they met, Jack attempted to sell him a couple of the pups.

"The grandest pups I've ever bred, Rabbi. Real classic looking, real champions, proper little Jewish pups they are."

But the Rabbi was not interested, so after a week had passed, Jack met the parish priest out for his evening stroll.

"Father," he said, "walking is a great healthy exercise, and no man walks further or happier than the one who has a greyhound at his side. Now, I have a beautiful litter of pups – perfect champions, innocent and kind, real Catholic pups."

Of course, the priest knew of Jack's attempt to sell the pups to the Rabbi.

"Jack," he said, "you offered them to the Rabbi last week and said that they were real Jewish pups. Now how do you explain that?"

But Jack was not stuck for an explanation.

"You are quite right, Father. I offered then to him a week ago, but their eyes are open now."

Bargain Hunter

"Maxine," said the loving husband, "I have seen the most beautiful ring costing five thousand pounds. I can get it for three thousand. Would you like it for your birthday?"

"No," replied the loving wife. "This year, give me the three thousand pounds and I'll choose my own present."

"And where do you think I could get three thousand pounds wholesale?" retorted the husband.

Mistaken Identity

He had been over in London for about three months and he was fed up and lonely. No friendly faces greeted him. The hustle and bustle was getting him down and he longed for the more relaxed days he had spent in the Irish countryside.

Then, walking down Oxford Street one day he casually glanced across to the other side of the street. He suddenly stopped. He could not believe his eyes for there, walking along, was his old school friend, Mick. Full of excitement, he shouted above the roar of the mighty London traffic, "Mick, Mick, it is me."

Sure enough, Mick heard him.

"Paddy," he shouted, "Paddy, me old friend, how are you?"

Simultaneously they dashed across the street to meet each other, and as they held out their hands for a big handshake they realised to their utter disappointment – it was neither of them.

The Good Samaritans

Maurice had enjoyed his holiday more than any other he had ever had.

He had been to Europe and America, but the peace and tranquillity of the Irish countryside, coupled with the friendliness of the people, had really impressed him.

On his return to London there was no doubt in his mind. He would sell up his business and open up in a country town in Ireland. Sure enough, he was true to his vow and in a few months the name "Maurice Shapiro – New and Secondhand Clothes Dealer" appeared over a vacant shop in Leighlin.

Business was good. Money was plentiful, and even the ones who bought on hire purchase never failed to turn up on Saturday with their weekly instalments. There was always a cheerful "Hello!" or "Fine day!" or "God be with you" from the country folk.

One Sunday, when out for a stroll, he met Brendan with whom he had a nodding acquaintance.

"Tell me, Brendan," he said, "why don't you come into my shop and we'll do some business together?"

"Begorrah," Brendan replied, "I could do with a new suit, but I wouldn't be able to pay cash for it."

"Not to worry, not to worry," Maurice said. "A small deposit, and you can pay me so much each Saturday for two years."

During the week Brendan signed on the dotted line, and left with a new suit such as he had never sported before. But, alas, to Maurice's surprise, Brendan did not arrive with his instalment the following week. However, Maurice did not take that too seriously. It was when Brendan failed to arrive the following week that he started to make enquiries regarding his customer.

"Brendan!" his informant exclaimed. "You gave Brendan credit? You must be mad. Sure he'd drink every shilling he could beg, borrow or steal."

But Maurice was not going to be put off that easily, so that Sunday he drove out to Brendan's house. He was shocked at what he saw – a tumbledown shack, neglected, and obviously occupied by somebody with little concern for personal standards and to whom forty pounds for a suit would be more of a joke than a luxury.

He banged loudly on the door but got no reply. However, a neighbour told him that he could expect Brendan home when the pubs shut.

Sure enough, in the afternoon Brendan came gaily singing along the lane. Maurice angrily approached him and demanded full payment there and then. Brendan laughed in his face.

"I don't intend paying you a penny," he said, "the suit is useless."

Confident that he could frighten him with the threat of the law, Maurice waved the hire purchase agreement in front of Brendan's eyes.

"You see that," he said. "It will cost you much more when I take you to court."

But apparently the threat of the law meant nothing to Brendan.

"Take me to court," he said, "take me to court. Everybody knows I've got nothing."

By this time Maurice realised that this line of approach would not succeed, and remembering that he had seen Brendan going to church on Sundays he thought that he would appeal to the religious side of his character.

"Surely," he said, "you have got some Christianity and that you know the story from the Bible when Jesus said, 'You were naked and I clothed you'."

But Brendan also knew his scripture.

"Ah," he said, "I agree, but remember 'You were a stranger and I took you in'."

Slow Coach

He was late for the market and was not sparing the ash plant on the donkey to make up for lost time. Suddenly a car pulled up in front of him and screeched to a halt. His eyes blazing with fury, the priest stepped out and savagely lashed Terence for his treatment of the animal.

"Do you know," he shouted, "that donkey is God's animal, or have you forgotten that it was on a donkey's back that Christ made the flight into Egypt? How dare you beat the poor dumb animal."

Terence looked at him in surprise.

"I agree with you, Father," he said. "But if he had been riding on this donkey of mine, He would never have got there."

The Historian

The school was breaking up for the summer holiday and Reverend Mother, the History teacher, was asking a few brief questions on what she had taught the pupils the previous year.

"Now," she said, "as a pleasant surprise I am going to give a fifty pence prize to the boy whom I consider gives the best answer to the following question: who was the most famous man in history?"

Johnny, the bright one, immediately jumped up.

"Julius Caesar," he said.

"A very famous man indeed," the Reverend Mother agreed. "Any other suggestions?"

This time Mick was on his feet.

"Napoleon," he said.

Again the Reverend Mother agreed. "A great man," she said. "Would anyone else like to give an answer?"

Next to stand up was David.

"Reverend Mother," he said, "I think Jesus Christ was the most famous man in history."

A broad smile lit up the teacher's face.

"Yes, David," she said, "*that* is the answer I was hoping for. He was indeed the greatest man in history. But tell me, as you are a little Jewish boy, shouldn't you believe that Moses was even greater?"

"Maybe I do," the little boy replied, "but fifty pence is fifty pence."

The Reunion

Rachel looked back on her times at school and felt lonely for her school chums. Two in particular, Becky and Ruth, had been great friends of hers, so she made enquiries as to their whereabouts and planned a get-together. She had done well in life and, of course, was proud of showing her friends her beautiful home.

When they arrived, they had a sumptuous meal and then retired to the sitting-room to talk about old and new times. They congratulated Rachel on her beautiful home.

"Yes," she said, "I have done well. My man, Hymie, is in the estate agency business. Last year his turnover was in the million bracket, and on five-per-cent commission that is a lot of money. Now, Becky, how have you been doing?"

Becky would not be outdone.

"Well," she said, "I have done well. My man, Sam, married me when he was an up-and-coming doctor. Now he is in Harley Street and has a long list of private patients – all titled. He employs three other doctors, and even his consultancy fee is five hundred guineas. At the very least he'll clear a couple of thousand pounds a week."

Everybody was delighted, and then it was Ruth's turn.

"Well, Ruth dear," Rachel asked, "now how have you done?"

"Well," Ruth replied, "I am perhaps the happiest woman in the world. You see, my husband is a Rabbi."

Rachel and Becky congratulated her warmly.

"Fancy being married to a Rabbi, you must be proud. But tell me," Becky asked, "what sort of money does he get in a year?"

Ruth smiled and said, "Oh, perhaps about eight hundred pounds a year."

Rachel looked at her in amazement and exclaimed, "Eight hundred pounds a year! What a funny job for a Yiddisher boy to take!"

The Family Painting

Seamus and his wife were spending a weekend in Dublin, and, having often heard reports of the beautiful sights to be seen in the Museum there, they decided to spend a few hours browsing around. Fascinated by the works of art, they gazed in awe at all the wonderful things that surrounded them.

Then the wonderful painting of *The Holy Family* by Da Vinci caught their eye. They went over and gazed at it in wonder and amazement. Silence reigned for about five minutes, and then the wife turned to Seamus and said, "We all know that they were poor, but when it came to having the family portrait done, you must agree they got the best artist available."

All Forgiven

Mrs Freedman was feeling alone in the world, and after a long day's work in the gown shop she was tired and weary. The biggest blow of all, however, was that the expected letter from her son, Peter, was not there when she got back to the flat.

He had emigrated to America the previous year and she hadn't heard from him for weeks. She made herself some coffee and decided to have an early night. And then the phone rang.

Wearily she picked it up and immediately recognised the voice.

"Peter!" she shouted, "Peter, my boy. How lovely to hear from you."

"Mother," Peter said, "I'm in New York for the day and I thought I'd surprise you. How are you, Mother?"

"Oh, great, Son. And how are you? Are you going to bed early?"

"Mother," the son replied, "I have a surprise for you – I'm coming home again next month."

Her joy was unbounded.

"Marvellous, marvellous!" she shouted. "It will be like old times. We'll have coffee and matzos and go to the synagogue on Saturday."

Here Peter interrupted.

"But, Mother," he started to say.

"Yes, Son," his mother queried.

Then he dropped the bombshell.

"I got married today."

It took a few seconds for the mother to grasp the full significance of this.

"I'm delighted, Son. I am so looking forward to seeing her, my little boy's wife."

"I hope you won't be disappointed, Mother," Peter said, "but she is an Irish girl and a Catholic."

For a little while there was silence and then she said, "And why should you not marry an Irish girl. After all, as Jewish people we cannot start to look down on other races. There are some good Irish people as well as some good Yiddisher people."

The next piece of the conversation was not so easy for her to accept.

"Mother," he said, "she is a divorced woman."

She was almost unable to reply, but decided to accept the *fait accompli*.

"Well," she said, "we live in changing times and I'm sure it was not her fault. So she made a mistake once. The main thing is that you love her and are happy with her."

Then came the final revelation.

"Mother," he said, "she has four children – two boys and two girls, and if you can accommodate us in the flat we will all arrive next week."

The mother was most enthusiastic.

"Of course you all can be accommodated. I've got it worked out already. You and the Irish woman can sleep in my room, the two boys can sleep in your old room, and the two girls can sleep in the spare room."

"But," Peter interrupted, "that's all the rooms in the flat. Where will you sleep?"

The mother's reply came quickly,

"Peter, my son, don't worry about me. When I leave down this phone, I'm going to drop dead."

Economics

When he was due to sit his final in Economics, Sean wrote to the University in Dublin asking if they would kindly forward to him the papers which were set for the previous two years' similar exams.

Within a few days he received them, and to his astonishment found that they included the questions for the examination he was about to sit. Looking more closely, he found that they were identical to the previous two years.

Realising that a serious slip had been made, he immediately sent the papers back with a covering letter explaining the error. However, by return of post he received a letter of thanks and appreciation of his honesty, but pointing out that the questions were in fact identical to previous years because it was considered by the country's leading economists that the economic problems were always the same and it was only the answers which changed yearly.

Business As Usual

The doctor said that he had a very short time to live.

"A matter of hours," he said sadly, "a matter of hours. If I were you, Mrs Levy, I would phone all the family."

Within half an hour they had all collected sadly at the bedside and with tear-stained eyes they had watched the old man growing weaker. Suddenly he opened his eyes, "Are you there, Becky?" he said.

"Yes, Dad," she said, "I'm here with you."

"God bless you," the old man said, "you were always a great comfort to me. And are you there, David?"

David did his best to console him and said, "Yes, Dad, I'm here with you and always will be."

A smile came over the old man's face and he asked again, "Are you there, Astor?"

"Yes, Dad," Astor said, "I'm here with you. Don't worry, none of us will leave you."

"So Becky is here, David is here, and Astor is here. The whole family is here with me."

Suddenly the patient sat bolt upright and his voice boomed out, "If you are all here, who the bloody hell is looking after the shop?"

Tactics

The instructor was lecturing forcibly on the discipline of Army life.

"I cannot stress too heavily the need to be always on your guard. In present day warfare," he said, "we have radar telecommunications, electronic devices, land mines, spotter planes, Sputniks, etc. to guard against surprise attack.

"And this is no innovation in war. If you read through history, you will find that the Greeks and Romans were always on their guard and they enlisted the aid of guard dogs, pitfalls, and even geese to alert them to sudden attack.

"The safety of an army, and maybe a nation, can depend on watchfulness and vigilance and, as you were taught at school, King Brian Boru was killed in his tent at the battle of Clontarf in 1014 through having no sentry outside.

"So, as you all can see, if he had had vigilant sentries, he might still be alive today."

Hind-Foresight

There had not been a spot of rain for months and the farmers were bemoaning their fate. Complete crop failure was inevitable, unless a miracle happened soon and a deluge arrived. However, Paddy and Mary still loved a stroll down the fields on a summer's evening, although the sight of the withering potato crops and corn saddened their hearts.

One evening, as they turned to come back to the farmhouse, the clouds suddenly darkened, a blinding flash of lightning swept across the field, and a bellowing clap of thunder rocked the countryside. Immediately the long awaited floodgates opened and the rain started to pour down as if some huge dam had burst. They couldn't believe their luck. Paddy threw his hat up towards the heavens and shouted out to his wife, "Mary, we are saved! An hour of that rain would do as much good in a day as a night of it would do in a week a month ago."

A Relative of the Groom

Brigit decided that she would devote her life to religion and piety and become a nun. Her parents were delighted, and all preparations were made for the great day when she would be professed.

During a shopping spree for the big event, her proud father explained to the local supermarket owner what was happening, but the owner, being Jewish, didn't fully understand.

"Tell me," he said, "what do you mean by being professed?"

Paddy explained in detail that Brigit was becoming a nun which, in effect, meant that she was renouncing all worldly pleasures and being married to the Lord. Hymie had never been to such an occasion as a profession, so he asked if he might come along to see the service.

The great day arrived and Hymie studied the ceremony with great interest, the placing of the wedding ring on her finger, the taking of the vows, etc. and was indeed very impressed with the sanctity of it all. On his way out of the church, one of the relatives whom he did not know was walking beside him. He introduced himself to Hymie, explaining that he was a cousin of the newly-professed nun, and then courteously asked, "Are you a relative? I don't think I've met you before."

Hymie, however, did not claim relationship, but said, "No, not exactly related. I'm the machatunim[4]."

---

[4] The groom's people.

The Phone Call

It was the biggest day in the life of the family, and Hymie and Becky had planned it for years. Their only son's Bar Mitzvah.

Then tragedy struck. The caterers, who were renowned for such occasions, were fully booked. In desperation Becky phoned the only other caterers in the district – Murphy and Sons.

"Of course, madam," Mr Murphy answered, "we will be delighted to do your son's Bar Mitzvah – and don't worry, we have a lot of experience in the field as we have catered for such occasions many times when we were in America. Just give me a list of the foods you want supplied and the number of guests, and you can happily leave the rest to us."

It was there and then agreed that the caterers would arrive in time to have the feast ready for the guests who were returning from Schule at 3 p.m. Becky felt relieved and Murphy and Sons duly arrived on time. On her return with the guests she looked into the banquet room and was delighted to see everything laid out to her highest expectations. But as the guests began to take their seats she noticed that there was something wrong.

"Mr Murphy," she said, "we are two places short."

But Mr Murphy was not in agreement.

"No, Mrs Cohen," he said. "There are thirty-eight guests and there are thirty-eight places."

Becky was outraged.

"I told you," she said, "that we had forty guests."

"Ah," Mr Murphy replied wisely, "but when you were away, a man phoned up and said the Beigels wouldn't be coming[5]."

---

[5] Beigels = Jewish bread rolls.

Racial Pride

Abie and Donal were discussing the relative contributions which the Irish and Jewish races had made to the world.

"What," said Abie, "has the Irish race to offer like Albert Einstein? This was a hundred-percent Jewish boy, a man who will live in history as one of the greats. A man who revolutionised the world of physics and maths. A man whose name will be forever mentioned where physicists and scholars gather."

"But," Donal commented, "what about Shackleton and his expedition? Surely his name will be honoured wherever ships sail and men of the sea gather? This was a hundred-percent Irish boy, and in the whole expedition there was not one Jewish connection."

Abie laughed.

"No Jewish connection," he said, "no Jewish connection, and tell me, where did they get the name *Iceberg*?"

The Economist

His doctor was fed up with Paul's constant visits to the surgery.

"Paul," he said, "I'm recommending you to a very good friend of mine – a psychiatrist. I can find nothing organically wrong with you."

So, handing his patient a name and address on a piece of paper, he said, "Your appointment is for Monday. Be there at 7 p.m. This is a very busy man."

Paul arrived on time, and after the usual formalities the psychiatrist invited him to sit on his couch.

"Well," he said, "your doctor has forwarded me your notes. I have studied them carefully, but I would like to know a few details about your private life – your hobbies, what you do in your spare time."

The patient felt completely relaxed.

"Well," he said, "I'm very fond of horse racing, and so I keep a small string of horses – about ten, I think – and I enjoy going to races when one of them is running. On weekends in summer I fly out to the Mediterranean in my small private plane with the family and enjoy a day's yachting. Some weekends I stay in England in my place in Devon – not a big place, just twenty acres of land and a Georgian house. My wife likes simple things, too. She has a Rolls of her own and likes to entertain perhaps twenty to thirty guests a few times each week. Our two sons are at Cambridge and our two girls at the Sorbonne. Apart from that I do very little."

"Well," said the psychiatrist, "it would appear that your problem is one of nervous tension. Tell me, is there anything worrying you?"

Paul replied, "I suppose I could say there is."

The psychiatrist pressed him further. "Please tell me about it. I must know all the facts if I am to help you."

"Well, you see," Paul replied, "I only earn £20 a week."

Blind Love

The Judge turned to the jury.

"Thank you, gentlemen, for your verdict. I agree with it completely, and in view of the gruesomeness of this case you are discharged from further jury service for life." He then turned to the two brothers in the dock.

"You have been correctly found guilty of an abominable attack on an old woman for a few pounds," he said sternly. "You are lucky that the doctors worked so hard or you might be standing before me on a far more serious charge. This was a premeditated and serious crime, and in view of its repulsiveness, and taking your past records into account, I have no hesitation in sentencing you both to the maximum penalty – twenty years hard labour."

There was a scream from the public gallery.

"My boys are not guilty, my boys could not have done it!"

Quickly the mother was hustled out of the court by an official, but she kept up her belief in their innocence.

Visiting time came round and she was first in the queue, demanding to see the Governor after she had visited her two sons.

"See me on the way out, madam," the warder said. "I will see if I can help you."

After the interview she seemed much happier and said so to Mrs O'Reilly, her neighbour, when she arrived home.

"Such a nice man the Governor is," she said. "He told me that they are first up every morning and keep themselves spotless. And the corridor shines like the sun coming up over the Wicklow mountains. Not a back answer has either of them given to any of the warders. They are two model prisoners, and he assured me that if they kept up this behaviour, they will get full remission of sentence and be out in twelve to fifteen years."

Mrs O'Reilly was delighted with the news.

"I'm so glad, Mrs Murphy," she said. "I bet you were proud when the Governor of the whole jail gave you the good news. Now aren't you the lucky woman to have two such well behaved boys!"

Well, Well

Andrew and Michael were experts at their jobs, and any farmer who wanted a running water supply to the house was glad to avail of their services. They would locate a spring in a field near by and sink a well hole. The rest was simple – install a pump and run a pipe to the house and the water could flow.

But this job was more difficult. The water supply was further down than usual and it took a long time to dig the hole. At last it was finished and they both looked at it with great pride.

"A fine job," Andrew commented.

Michael agreed.

"It must be about thirty feet deep."

"Could be more," Andrew suggested, and as if to confirm his remark, he leaned over and looked down. And then it happened . . . He lost his balance and crashed down the hole. Michael was panic stricken.

"Are you all right, Andrew?" he shouted.

Back came the reply, "Of course I am all right."

But Michael was not satisfied.

"Did you break anything?" he shouted and was totally relieved when Andrew replied, "Don't be such a bloody fool. There's nothing down here to break."

Great Expectations

Larry was returning from the market where he had sold the fat pig when he saw his neighbour Patricia leaning over her front gate. She was known as the most inquisitive woman in the district and sure enough, as he passed, she started her questioning.

"Been to the market then?" she commented.

He had to agree.

"A good day then, was it?" she asked.

"Aye, fairly good," he replied.

"What were the prices like?" she further inquired.

"Fairly good," came the reply.

"Well you got a good price then?" she further asked.

"Well, I did and I didn't," was his answer.

"I hope you got what you expected?" she questioned.

Larry had the final word.

"No," he said, "I didn't get what I expected but I didn't expect I would!"

Living Out

Hymie had retired from business. He was indeed a very, very wealthy man. His greatest joy in life now was his grandson, and all his time was spent making plans for the boy's future.

Then the great day of the boy's Bar Mitzvah arrived. The grandfather approved any present that the boy might plan for.

"Come, my boy," he said, "we will go into London and anything you want you can have."

They walked through all the shops but nothing impressed the boy until, going down Oxford Street, he suddenly stopped and said, "Grandad, what a marvellous store."

He was looking at Selfridges.

"If you like it, my boy, I'll buy it for you," replied Hymie.

And so the old man went up to one of the shop assistants and asked, "I want to buy this place – whom do I see?"

The assistant looked at him in amazement.

"Excuse me, sir, but *this* is Selfridges."

"Selfridges, Selfridges. Take me to the Manager," Hymie said.

The assistant obliged and took Hymie to the Manager. Hymie stated the nature of his mission.

"I want to buy this place as a Bar Mitzvah present for my grandson."

The Manager smiled.

"Do you know you are talking about Selfridges, one of the biggest stores in London. It is valued at around fifty million pounds!"

"Fifty million pounds, sixty million pounds," Hymie said. "If my boy wants it, he can have it."

Realising that he was dealing with a very rich man, the Manager decided to be courteous.

"All right, sir, would you like to look around?"

Hymie agreed and they visited all the various departments on all the different floors. When they had visited the last department, Hymie said, "Now, can I see the living quarters?"

The Manager looked at him in amazement.

"The living quarters? The *living* quarters? Good gracious, there are no living quarters in Selfridges."

Hymie threw his hands up to the sky.

"No living quarters?" he despaired. "You want fifty million pounds for a blooming gunza lock-up?"

Late Arrival

The plane had just taken off from Dublin Airport on its flight to London, and Paddy was filled with excitement at the thought of his new life in the city. The flight captain's voice came over the microphone.

"Welcome aboard, ladies and gentlemen. This is to tell you that our arrival in London will be delayed by about twenty minutes. One of the engines has packed up, but this, of course, is nothing at all to worry about. We have three perfectly good engines left, but as I said we will be about twenty minutes late arriving. You may unfasten your safety belts and you can smoke, and I hope you will enjoy the trip."

Paddy sat back, relaxed, and lit a cigarette. But before long the captain's voice again interrupted.

"Ladies and gentlemen," he said, "this is the captain speaking. This is a brief announcement to tell you that we have had some trouble with the second engine. You may notice that the engine sound has changed slightly. There is, however, no need at all for alarm. We have two perfectly good engines left, but unfortunately we will be about three-quarters of an hour late in arriving at London Airport."

Paddy continued to puff his cigarette and enjoy the view of the channel below. But again the captain's voice came over.

"Ladies and gentleman," he said, "I am sorry to keep interrupting. This is briefly to tell you that the third engine has packed up, but there is no need to worry. We have one perfectly good engine left. Unfortunately, however, we will be two hours late in arriving at London Airport. I am indeed sorry for the delay and hope that it will not inconvenience you too much."

Paddy was not quite happy about the announcement this time. He turned to the passenger beside him and said, "Jesus, if the fourth engine packs up we will be up here all night."

Divine Revenge

It was dawn on the Saturday morning and Hymie lay awake listening to the song of the birds in the nearby golf course. He was a keen golfer himself and the urge to play a game became stronger and stronger, but then it was the Sabbath Day, a day of self-denial and holiness. But as the light of the sun came through his window the call of the golf course became too great, so he decided to have a game. After all, at this early hour nobody would see him, and his secret would be safe.

However, to the watchful eyes of Heaven the world is indeed a small place, and scarcely had he arrived at the golf course when he came under the notice of Holy St Peter. The Saint looked down on Hymie in horror and dismay. No sin could be more grave to the Rabbi than to indulge in pleasure on the Sabbath Day. St Peter quickly made his way to the office of the Lord.

"Lord," he said, "have you seen what Rabbi Cohen is up to?"

"I have indeed," replied the Lord, "but rest assured, he will be heavily punished."

Meanwhile the Rabbi prepared to tee off. He steadied himself and took a swing. It was a beautiful stroke and the ball went straight to the hole and, to the Rabbi's utter amazement, went straight in. He threw his golf club in the air and danced a merry dance.

Far away up in Heaven St Peter turned to the Lord.

"Lord," he said, "there seems to be something wrong. You promised that he would be severely punished for his sin, but instead you have allowed him to achieve every golfer's dream – a hole in one!"

The Lord looked at him wryly.

"I agree, Peter, he said, "he *has* achieved a hole in one, but whom can he tell?"

Blind Faith

Cliff climbing was their hobby and Mick and Paddy were experts. One day they had got about two-thirds up the face of a very steep cliff about six thousand feet high. Suddenly Paddy missed a step and went crashing towards his death in the sea four thousand feet below. Mick looked on in horror as his good friend disappeared. Luckily, however, Paddy remained conscious, and to his enormous relief he saw a tree branch protruding in his path. As a drowning man grasps at a straw he grabbed the branch and hung on for dear life.

Realising his terrible position, he could only put faith in the Lord for his rescue.

"Oh, heavens above," he cried in anguish, "if there is anybody there, save me."

Immediately a voice boomed out, "Have faith, my child, and do as you are told. Close your eyes, trust in me, and let go your hold on the branch."

Mick quickly closed his eyes as if to obey the instructions. Then he had second thoughts.

"Is there anybody else there?" he shouted back.

Chutspa *(a hard neck)*

"I am horrified," the Judge said, "at this horrible crime, and even more so by the fact that you are a Jewish boy. You belong to a race of people who seldom, if ever, indulge in acts of criminal violence, and to whom the closeness and love of family life is one of their proudest possessions.

"Your parents devoted their hard-working lives to you. You have been given an excellent rearing, a first class education. You were sent to the best schools your unfortunate parents could afford, and yet, despite all this, you caused their deaths. I cannot even find an excuse, although I have searched through all the evidence for a mitigating circumstance which would slightly justify this crime against your people and the good name of your race. So consequently I intend to impose the maximum sentence which the law decrees. I know of no reason why your sentence should be less than the maximum. If you know of any reason for mitigation, you are at liberty to say so."

"Surely," the prisoner replied, "I can plead for leniency on the grounds that I am an orphan."

Research Rewarded

A question which has remained unanswered for many years has at last been resolved in Dublin.

Who wrote the famous works? Was it really William Shakespeare or was it Bacon or Marlowe or even Kydd, or who?

Scientists, doctors, actors, writers and an assortment of intellectuals decided that the time had come for thorough investigation of the mystery. All his works were read and re-read for a clue, Stratford was revisited, and even Anne Hathaway's cottage was searched from floor to roof. The excitement was tremendous and it was even rumoured that a certain football manager asked to be informed if, by any chance, he was found to have an Irish grandfather.

After months of study the world awaited the final outcome. The press and other media assembled when the chairman made his shattering announcement that after long and thorough study it was unanimously agreed that it was *not* William Shakespeare who wrote the plays – it was another man of the same name.

Not To Worry

For about a month he had not slept well at night. He was kicking and twisting in the bed. Eventually it reached such heights that his wife could stand it no longer.

"Abie, Abie, tell me what's the trouble. Why can't you sleep?"

Abie was adamant not to discuss it and said, "There's no point in telling you. I *have* got trouble but you can't help."

His wife, however, insisted.

"Abie," she said, "we are husband and wife. We must share our troubles. Tell me, because I can probably help you."

After much persuasion Abie relented.

"Alright," he said, "I borrowed one hundred pounds from Zachie across the street. I must pay him back in the morning, and I simply have not got the money. Now didn't I tell you that you could not help me, and now you will worry about it as well."

"Oh no," the wife said, "I can help you, so stop worrying. I can deal with this."

"You mean you have a hundred pounds?"

"No," she said, "I have not got a hundred pence, but don't worry – leave it to me."

She jumped out of bed, put on her dressing gown and slippers, and went across the street to Zachie's house. She banged heavily on the door, and after a while Zachie put his head out of the window.

"Do me a favour, what do you want at this hour of the morning?"

"My husband owes you a hundred pounds," she said, "and he can't sleep with worry because he hasn't got the money to give you. So now he is going to sleep and it's your turn to stay awake and worry."

Progress

The tourists were enjoying a conducted tour of Dublin. The guide knew his history and duly pointed out the places of international interest.

"This is Guinness' Brewery, the biggest brewery in the world."

There was, however, one dissenting voice – a cigar-smoking Texan.

"Gee," he said, "do you call that thing big! We have bakeries in Texas ten times as big as that thing."

Paddy did not comment and the tour continued.

Next stop was the GPO with its beautiful arches and wonderful architecture.

"This," Paddy said with pride, "is the biggest post office in Ireland."

Before he could go any further the Texan's voice again intervened.

"The biggest in Ireland," he laughed. "Boy, we have lavatories in Texas bigger than that, and we built them overnight."

The next stop was Nelson's monument. Paddy was sure that he would score here.

"This," he said proudly, "is Nelson's Monument, the tallest monument in Ireland. It took three years to build."

Again the Texan intervened.

"The tallest monument?" he laughed. "Why, the farmers in Texas have taller scarecrows and they build them in an hour."

Paddy again did not reply, and the tour continued towards the Customs House. As the bus was about to pull up, the Texan looked out of the window and said.

"Gee, at long last I must agree you really have something in Dublin – *that* is a fabulous building; tell me all about it."

Paddy scratched his head and looked at the Texan, "I'm afraid I can't, sir," he said. "It wasn't there when I was going to work this morning."

A Fishy Story

Paddy and Manny were great pals, and one day Paddy decided that he too would expand his business as his friend had done, and become somebody in the world of finance. When they met, he said, "Manny, do me a favour and tell me something. Why is it that Jewish people are so successful in business?"

Manny shook his head.

"Paddy," he said, "you are one of my best friends, but you are asking too much now. I cannot let you in on the secret."

But Paddy persisted. Finally, Manny gave in.

"All right," he said, "I'll tell you, but on your life you must never tell anybody. It's a certain type of fish we eat that gives us brains."

This information, of course, was of very little use to Paddy unless he could obtain the fish.

"Well," Paddy said, "I have a deal coming off next week. Would you ever bring me a fish, I'll pay you well for it."

Sure enough, next evening Manny arrived with a fish measuring about three feet in length. Paddy was delighted.

"Thanks a million, Manny," he said. "How much?"

"To you, Paddy, two pounds," replied his friend.

Paddy paid him promptly, and, after giving him all the instructions about preparation and cooking, Manny left.

Sure enough, the business deal was very successful and Paddy was enthralled. He decided to go in for bigger things and again approached his friend.

"Manny," he said, "I have an even bigger deal coming off next week. Could you get me another fish?"

Manny agreed and arrived that night with a fish measuring about two feet. Once again Paddy was delighted.

"Thanks, Manny," he said, "thanks. How much?"

"Five pounds," Manny replied.

Paddy raised no objection and paid him on the spot. Once again his deal was successful and so he decided to go in for the big kill. But first he had to ensure another supply of the brain-giving fish. He went to Manny's house and Manny agreed that he would deliver a fish that evening.

He arrived with a fish in due course. This time the fish measured about one foot in length. Paddy was delighted.

"How much, Manny?" he asked.

Manny looked at him sternly.

"Ten pounds," he said.

But this time Paddy was not so forthcoming.

"Manny," he said, "I don't understand this. The first fish you gave me was three foot long and you charged me two pounds. The second fish was only two foot long and you charged me five pounds. Now you have brought me a fish one foot long and you want ten pounds for it!"

Manny agreed completely.

"You are right, Paddy," he said. "But you must agree that it works. You got brains already!"

Diplomacy

Jack was fast approaching late middle age. His father had died some years previously, but his mother was still fighting fit. She was a great housekeeper, but despite the best of home comforts there was one thing that Jack was missing – a wife.

Many times he tried to discuss the matter with his mother, but she proved very difficult.

"Don't you think you have plenty of time to spare before even thinking of marriage?" she would say. "And what more do you want for the present? Your meals are cooked for you, your shirts are washed and ironed, and the house is spotless. Talk to me about it in ten years' time."

Jack knew he would never convince her. And then he had an idea. He would talk to the parish priest, Father Colm, and get his advice.

The priest saw his point of view straight away.

"I'll see what I can do, Jack," he said. "It's sometimes difficult to get parents to agree to a young wife taking over where they have reigned for years," he continued.

"Now, let me see, what Mass will you be at on Sunday?"

Jack and his mother always went to Midday Mass and he told the priest so.

"Good," the priest replied. "I will be saying that Mass, so make sure that you and your mother sit near the pulpit and I will give the sermon on the sanctity and blessing of marriage."

Jack made certain that he and his mother were early for Mass and that they took their seats as the priest had directed. They listened to a beautiful sermon on life in general and on marriage in particular.

"It's a social and Christian obligation for young people to get married," the preacher said. "To marry young, so that they have youth and strength to bring up their children in the fear and love of God, and not only that, but it is selfish to deny the grandparents the wonderful opportunity to see their family line continue in the grandchildren. But alas, occasionally a mother or father may be so selfish as to object to a son or daughter marrying. This is a mean and sinful outlook. I will emphasise the Words of the Good Book: '*Go forth and multiply*'."

Jack was delighted. If these words did not convince his mother, nothing in the world would.

So, when Mass was ended, his step was light as, with his mother, he set out for home. But the mother was strangely silent. Jack decided he would broach the subject of the sermon.

"What did you think of Father Colm's sermon, Mother?" he asked.

The mother looked at him with a painful and guilty look on her face.

"Jack," she said, "may God forgive me. It's a cause of confession but, would you believe it, as soon as the priest started to preach, I dozed off to sleep and never opened my eyes until he finished. Tell me, what was he talking about?"

Excelsior

They met on a train. You know how it is on these occasions – there are only two of you in the compartment and soon you are talking like old friends. Maybe the subject is the weather, as it usually is in Ireland, but this time it was children.

"A lovely little boy," Hymie agreed, looking at the photograph, "and what do you intend to prepare him for in life?"

"Please God," Paddy replied. "One day the Missus and myself will see him ordained a priest."

There was intonation in his voice which implied that no further discussion was necessary. But Hymie did not take the hint.

"Paddy," he asked, "how far can a priest get in your church?"

Paddy was amazed at the question.

"What on earth do you mean?" he asked. "Isn't being a priest all that the heart of a man can desire?"

"True enough," Hymie agreed, "but if he were my boy and entering a profession, I'd make sure there were promotional prospects. Can your boy reach no higher than an ordinary priest?"

"Prospects, prospects," Paddy shouted. "Well, if you insist on knowing, I'd die happy if I saw him a parish priest."

"A parish priest," said Hymie. "Is that the limit? On my life, I'm not being offensive but I'd like to know."

It seemed a reasonable question to Paddy, and with the missionary spirit welling up in him he said, "Well, he could become a bishop."

"A bishop, a bishop," said Hymie. "Now *that* sounds better. And that's the highest rank obtainable, is it?"

"Oh no," said Paddy. "If he was holy enough and it was the will of God, he could become an archbishop."

"Well," Hymie said, "I hope he does become an archbishop and reach the top."

Paddy marvelled at his ignorance.

"Don't misunderstand me," he said patiently, "there is a higher rank – a cardinal."

"And wouldn't you like your boy to become a cardinal?" Hymie suggested.

Paddy's face beamed.

"Cardinal Patrick Murphy," he said. "Cardinal Patrick Murphy. Wouldn't it be the proud day for his mother and myself kneeling for his blessing."

"That, of course, is the highest he can go in the Catholic religion," Hymie remarked.

That was too much for Paddy.

"You ignorant heathen," he exploded. "Have you never heard of his Holiness the Pope?"

"Of course, of course," Hymie replied, "I have heard of him. He lives in Rome, doesn't he? But tell me, why couldn't your boy become Pope?"

Paddy pitied his ignorance.

"Of course he could become Pope. You don't have to be Italian to be Pope, but few people would cherish such a dream."

"I'm pleased to hear you say that any nationality can become Pope. That shows that there must be no racial prejudice among religious orders," Hymie replied. "But tell me, my friend, is a Pope the highest rank in the Catholic Church?"

That was the last straw for Paddy. He crashed his fist down and shouted, "And what do you want my son to be – Jesus Christ Himself?"

Hymie shrugged his shoulders.

"I believe one of our lads was," he said.

Ad Infinitum

God decided that he would act as intermediary in the Middle East troubles and so he called together the three most troubled men from that area – Mr Yasser Arafat, Mr Sadat, and Mr Begin.

"Now," He said, "I will give each of you an answer to the question which is troubling you most in life. Mr Yasser Arafat – you are first. What is your question?"

Mr Yasser Arafat came straight to the point. "Dear God," he said, "tell me in which year I will find the homeland for my Palestinian refugees?"

God replied immediately, "In the year 2226."

Mr Yasser Arafat burst into tears. "I shall never see it," he mobbed. "I shall be long long dead."

God now turned to Mr Sadat. "Mr Sadat," He said, "what is the most important question troubling you?"

"Tell me, dear God," said Mr Sadat, "in what year will I be able to demobilise my huge Egyptian army, industrialise my country, and live in peace?"

Again God replied instantly, "In the year 2648."

Mr Sadat burst into tears. "I will be dead," he said. "I will never see it."

Finally God turned to Mr Begin, who was ready with his question.

"Tell me, dear God," he said, "in what year will I be able to conquer inflation in Israel?"

And God burst into tears.

The First Lesson of History

With his wife and four children Solly had lived eight long years in one small room in Dublin, and his various applications to the council for rehousing had brought no reply.

Then one morning, looking through his solitary window, he saw a removal van parked in the street opposite, and Mick, the downstairs tenant, loading his belongings. Solly decided that he would investigate and was amazed to find that Mick had been rehoused in a new council flat.

"I can't understand it, Mick," he said. "I've got a wife and four kids and have been in this room for eight years, and I can't get rehoused. You have a wife, one child and three rooms, yet after six months you are getting a new flat."

Mick was full of sympathy.

"Solly, would you mind answering me a personal question? When you fill in your application for a flat, what religion do you enter on the form?"

"Jewish, of course," Solly replied automatically.

"Ah well," Mick said, "I don't think you stand much chance if you continue to do that. Take my advice, fill in another form and enter your religion as Roman Catholic – it may make a difference."

Solly took his advice, and within a couple of weeks received a letter from the Housing Department to come for interview regarding rehousing. Full of trepidation, he arrived at the council offices at the appointed time and was directed into the office of the Housing Manager who was sitting holding the application form that Solly had sent in. He received a friendly welcome and was made to feel at ease.

"Mr Cohen," the manager commenced, "I am shocked to learn of the conditions under which you and your family have been living for eight years, and I shall make a point of finding out why this matter has not been attended to before now. You have a wife and four children?"

Solly nodded in agreement.

"On your form," the Housing Manager said, "you have given your religion as Roman Catholic, so would you mind if I asked you a few questions?"

Solly agreed.

"Can you tell me then, Mr Cohen, who started the Roman Catholic religion?"

Quickly Solly replied, "Jesus Christ."

The Housing Manager nodded in agreement. "Tell me," he asked, "where did He institute the religion?"

Solly was on the ball once again and replied, "In Israel, sir."

"Tell me," came the further question, "where was Jesus born?"

Solly had the answer to that one too. "In a stable in Bethlehem," he said.

"One last question, Mr Cohen. Can you tell me why Jesus was born in a stable?"

Solly was not quite so quick with his answer to this one. He scratched his head for a while and then said, "I am not one hundred percent sure, sir, but I would imagine it was because his mother and father were Jewish and they couldn't get a council house."

Tact

The German diplomat was making his first visit to Israel, and when informed that he was being taken on a tour of the Thomas Mann Memorial Hall, he felt that it was an indication that some of the cracks in the two countries' relationships were gradually healing.

Naturally he was all praise for the new structure and remarked to his guide how delighted he was that such a building should be called after a famous German writer. He was a little taken aback, however, when he was informed that the building was named in honour of Thomas Mann, an American writer.

Trying not to seem out of touch with the art world, he tactfully enquired what that particular author had written.

The Israeli smiled knowingly, and replied, "A cheque."

The Humble One

The Jesuits were giving a two weeks mission in the town. Parishioners from far and near gathered to hear the sermons, for the Jesuits are famous for their power of oratory.

Amongst the congregation was a Capuchian father from a nearby monastery. The Capuchian, the keynote of whose order is humility, listened in awe to the words of wisdom which flowed from the preacher's lips. So impressed was he that when the service was completed, he felt that he had to congratulate the Jesuit on his performance.

"Father Jesuit," he said, "I feel that I must congratulate you on that wonderful sermon. In all my years in the religious life never have I seen a congregation so moved. But then," he continued, shaking his head, "nobody of course can preach like a Jesuit. However," he said, sticking out his chest, "when it comes to humility, nobody, but *nobody*, can equal the Capuchians."

The Dead Loser

A group of archaeologists were at work in Israel and were astounded to discover an old coffin deep down in the earth. Gently they raised it to the surface and were amazed, after wiping the lid clean, to read the words:

HERE LIES RALPH GOLDSTEIN, THE FIRST JEWISH SUICIDE

All excited they gently prised open the lid, and there beheld a skeleton such as they had never seen before. The facial bones were twisted in an expression of rage and disappointment and his hands were firmly clenched by his sides. Looking closer, the team noticed that one hand contained a piece of paper still intact over the many centuries. Slowly and with great care they forced the hand open and discovered the paper was in fact a betting slip on which was written his last bet: *"Five hundred shekels to win, Goliath."*

Marital Bliss

An important part of a marriage was the first Sunday at Mass – when the whole parish took a good look at the new bride.

Important too was the journey there. The pony and trap must be looking their best, but alas, Jo had a very aged and worn out pony, so he decided that he would have to buy a younger one for the occasion. After a lot of haggling with the travelling people, he did so. Experience had proven that these roadside dealers did not supply the most trustworthy of stock. However, this one seemed to fit the job, and the deal was made.

Come Sunday morning, Jo yoked the pony to the trap. He and Maura, his newly wedded wife, sat in, and the usual command was passed to the pony: "Go on!"

But the animal showed his displeasure by giving the bottom of the trap a resounding kick. Jo was furious and, waving a large stick at the pony's head, he shouted, "That's once!"

A mile or two down the road they overtook a neighbour walking to Mass and offered him a lift, which was gladly accepted. The command to "Go on" was repeated and, as before, the pony gave a resounding kick to the trap before moving on its way. Jo was even more furious and, waving the stick towards the pony's head, he shouted, "That's twice!"

The journey proceeded normally until they reached the church where the pony was tethered to the railings until Mass ended, and Jo and his wife returned for the journey home. After having untied the pony they both took their seats. Jo again issued his instructions, "Go on!"

This time the pony was even more rebellious and gave the trap a much harder kick. That was too much for Jo. He jumped out of the trap, stood in front of the unfortunate animal, and hit him on the forehead with all his strength. The poor animal collapsed. Maura was astounded.

"Ah, Jo!" she shouted.

But Jo would brook no reproach. In a flash he was standing in front of his wife. He waved the stick in front of her forehead and shouted at the top of this voice, "That's once!"

And they lived happily ever after.

Chanukah Gift

It is customary during the feast of Chanukah[6] to present the younger generation with gifts, but Rabbi Broder was puzzled when his son asked him for the gift of a Honda.

An orthodox Jew, he was very confused indeed.

He simply didn't know the meaning of the word and could not recollect having come across it in the Torah. Always diplomatic, he explained to his son that he would think it over.

Later that day he phoned his friend Rabbi Mayor, who was of the Reformist Congregation, but he got no help from that quarter. Rabbi Mayor could not recollect the word as being in any of his teachings, but suspected that it might be some modern terminology which the liberal Rabbi Jacobs could explain.

Rabbi Broder phoned him immediately and was surprised to learn that a Honda was simply the name of a Japanese motorcar or motorcycle.

"I am surprised," he said, "that you didn't know the meaning of the word 'Honda'. But now can I ask a question, Rabbi Broder? What's Chanukah?"

---

[6] The feast of light.

Miscellany

Translations

Latin: Puto ergo sum.
English: I think, therefore I am.
Irish: I think, therefore I am, I think.

In Memoriam

Here lies Margaret Bridget, beloved wife of Sam Casey, died nineteen hundred and fifty-four. You are lost forever in your eternal sleep. Tears cannot restore thee, therefore I weep.

This stone was erected in memory of James Murphy, killed in action, and his brother Michael, drowned at sea. Had he lived, he would have been buried here.

Philosophy

One man is as good as another, and a damn sight better.

And then he grew so popular that nobody liked him.

It takes all kinds to make a world, and thank God I am not one of them.

Don't believe too much in happiness – learn to be happy without it.